JAMES VELLA-BARDON is the author
of several books to date, including
The Cream of Chivalry and *A Rebel North*.
His debut, *The Sheriff's Catch*, was the winner
in the 'best novel' and 'best historical fiction' categories at the International Royal Dragonfly Book Awards 2019.

"The new king of historical fiction"
– *The Scotsman*

"Remember the name of rising author
James Vella-Bardon"
– *Reader's Digest*

"Reminds me of works by today's masters such as
Bernard Cornwell, Conn Iggulden and Wilbur Smith"
– *Yorkshire Evening Post*

"Has what it takes to become a literary giant"
– *The Star*

"Sheer quality, historical integrity
and emotional resonance"
– *The London Economic*

MAD KING ROBIN

The Mad Shall Inherit The Earth

James Vella-Bardon

Tearaway Press

TEARAWAY PRESS

Copyright

Published by Tearaway Press 2022
PO Box 477, Belrose West, Sydney NSW 2085

Copyright © James Vella-Bardon 2022
Second edition © 2023

James Vella-Bardon asserts the moral right to be identified
as the author of this work.

ISBN: 978-0-6451230-3-6

Cover design and typesetting by Rafael Andres

To an uncle and a nephew, in any given time
and place throughout history, both mad enough to take on the odds

CONTENTS

Cover

Dedication

Title Page

Prologue – SACRILEGE

Chapter I – STIRLING

Chapter II –THE HOSTAGE

Chapter III – THE PLOY

Chapter IV – THE DUEL

Chapter V – RANDOLPH'S REDEMPTION

Chapter VI – THE VISITORS

Chapter VII – ALEXANDER

Chapter VIII - BANNOCKBURN

Chapter IX – REUNION

Historical Note

Acknowledgements

About The Author

Dramatis Personae

The Scots

King Robert I of Scotland (the Bruce)

Elizabeth de Burgh, Queen of Scotland

Eideard Bruce, Earl of Carrick

Sir James Douglas, Lord of Douglas (the Black Douglas)

Thomas Randolph, Earl of Moray

Angus *Óg* MacDonald, Lord of the Isles

Philip Mowbray, Governor of Stirling Castle

The English

King Edward II of England

Aymer de Valence, Earl of Pembroke and the king's lieutenant in Scotland

Humphrey de Bohun, Earl of Hereford, Constable of England

Gilbert de Clare, Earl of Gloucester, commander of the English vanguard

Robert de Clifford, Baron de Clifford and Lord Warden of the Marches

Sir Henry de Bohun, an English knight

The Dead

Sir William Wallace, Guardian of Scotland

John Comyn III, Lord of Badenoch (the Red)

King Edward 'Longshanks' I of England

Piers Gaveston, an English nobleman of Gascon origin and the favourite of King Edward II of England

"...Our humbleness has led us, now and at other times, to beseech your highness more devoutly so that, having God and public decency in sight, you would take pains to cease from our persecution and the disturbance of the people of our kingdom in order that devastation and the spilling of a neighbour's blood may henceforth stop..."

being an excerpt of a letter from King Robert I of Scotland to King Edward II of England, 1 October 1310

SACRILEGE

The small window glowed in the light of the dying sun. It was a small dome-shaped aperture, situated high above a large crucifix. A weak radiance streamed through it, revealing an intricate marble floor which spread before an oaken door that creaked open. A faint gust of wind blew across the nave, which disturbed the flames of the nine candles behind the altar. The overbearing silence in the chapel was broken by a man dressed in a fur-lined cloak. As he stepped inside he wore a frown on his face, and his long red hair was parted in the middle. The entrant's breathing was terse as he closed the door before he proceeded to enter the circle of faint light before him.

'Times are troubled indeed, Lord of Badenoch, if you must also bear arms in a place of worship.'

The redheaded lord jerked his head to the right. Across the nave he could make out a tall figure kneeling before a statue of the Holy Virgin, with both palms tightly clasped together in prayer.

'Hail, Robert the Bruce,' said the redheaded lord with a sneer.

It was a dismissive salutation, for the Bruce should have been greeted as the Earl of Carrick. Yet there was no love lost between the two men, so that the slight was repaid in kind.

'Hail, John the Red,' replied the still kneeling figure, 'and well met. I am here, just as we agreed.'

The Bruce rose to his feet and bowed once to the statue of the Madonna, before walking towards the newcomer. John the Red quietly observed his approach, then decided to further assess the Bruce's mood by engaging in further conversation.

'Word reached us from London that Longshanks wants you dead,' said the Red, while beads of perspiration prickled his brow despite the winter cold.

In truth the tidings from England had filled the Red with a deep joy. Yet he was still nervous, for he knew that one did not lightly cross Robert the Bruce. Which was not to say that the Red had lightly crossed the Bruce, because he had recently done far worse than that. For years, great rivalry had existed between John the Red Comyn and Robert the Bruce. For after the king of Scotland had died childless, both men held a claim to the Scottish throne.

Robert the Bruce and John Comyn were each thirty-one years of age, yet had the wisdom of men twice their age. From their earliest years, they were both forced to take part in battles and eventually also lead their own armies. Both men were once also the Guardians of Scotland, yet many arguments had often broken out between them during the gatherings of Scottish lords.

So John the Red was surprised when the Bruce had agreed to enter into a secret pact with him. This agreement bound the Red to support any Bruce-led revolt against Longshanks, the fearsome English king, who constantly behaved as if he were Lord Paramount of Scotland. Yet in truth the pact had been a cunning ploy by the Red to destroy his lifelong rival. Indeed, Comyn was surprised that the Bruce was still alive at all.

The Bruce stepped into the glowing circle on the marble floor, standing around five paces from his visitor. On his part the Red was also quietly delighted to see that recent days had not been kind to his young rival. For the Bruce was swathed in a fraying cloak which hid all of his appearance save for his height, which exceeded that of most men. The Bruce pulled back the hood about his head with blistered fingers, revealing gaunt and unkempt features beneath an unruly tangle of brown locks.

As the Red observed the Bruce's weary countenance, he became more confident. As he became more confident, he was also overcome by hatred so that his initial wariness turned into a growing rage. Meanwhile the Bruce maintained a stern, unmoving expression as he reached for something in his cloak. At this gesture, a low intake of breath was heard from the Red, who took a step backwards.

'Why Lord Comyn,' whispered the Bruce, 'do you not trust me?'

The Red flinched when the Bruce threw something towards his feet, which produced a sharp clink of steel against stone. The Lord of Badenoch scowled at the coins and the steel spurs which had landed upon the ground before him.

'What is that?' he snapped.

'Twelve pence and a pair of spurs,' replied the Bruce. 'A trusted friend sent them to me in London, the day after Longshanks interrogated me about our pact.'

'I see,' replied the Red between gritted teeth.

He felt crushed by disappointment, while secretly cursing the man who had warned the Bruce about Longshanks' intentions.

'I rode my unhappy steed half to death to flee England,' said the Bruce.

The Red said nothing while the Bruce whipped out a scroll and held it out before him.

'Here is our pact. You agreed to support my claim for kingship in return for the Scottish king's lands. Now that Longshanks has learned of it, he will invade. The hour is at hand. The time has come for us to rise up again. Together we can be free again.'

At the Bruce's declaration, the Red stared back at him defiantly while his lips formed into a smirk.

'I will do no such thing,' he said, never batting an eyelid as he enjoyed the changing expressions on his rival's face.

The Bruce's expression had already changed from one of shock to one of disbelief. As he stared back at the Red, he eventually sighed and looked wholly crestfallen as the scroll fell from his hand onto the floor.

'Why did you do it, John?' he asked at last. 'The pact was your idea.'

The Red appeared thrilled by the Bruce's dismay, with his rage welling up further as he stepped towards his old rival.

'Do not look at me like that, Bruce. You who have only ever served your own interests, who have only raised your sword for or against Scotland as best suited you.'

'You are not Scotland,' whispered the Bruce. 'And yet I would have given you whatever you wanted. We had a pact.'

'And more fool you for believing in it!' roared the Red, his eyes blazing from his years of hatred for the Bruce. 'Who are you, for me to be second to you? After all, my claim to the throne is the rightful one. You thought that I would surrender it to you so readily?'

In his anger the Red stopped short of seizing the Bruce by the throat, as he had infamously done years earlier. On his part Robert did not stir as John Comyn yelled at him again.

'Wallace, Moray, my uncle, me – we all bled for this land! All of us more loved by the people than you, who would as readily fight for Longshanks and swan about his court! Men say he once all but considered you his own son!'

Spittle dribbled down the Red's chin as his livid stare bore into the Bruce who beheld him almost sorrowfully.

'Readily do you talk of fighting for freedom!' yelled Comyn, 'yet did you end up in the tower of London, like I did? Did you beg at the king of France's feet for this land's freedom?' Tell me, lord Robert, what did you ever do to earn the right to become king? When did *you* bleed? How did *you* suffer?'

The Red was appalled when the Bruce spoke again, seemingly deaf to all of his rival's accusations.

'I thought you were a man of honour.'

'Honour be damned!' shouted the Red, then laughed aloud, 'I have freed Scotland from a profiteer and a would-be usurper. And now Scotland will no longer be divided, for Longshanks wants you torn apart. You are finished Robert, yet there was only ever one true heir to the throne.'

He turned on his heel and readied to make for the door.

'And you think Longshanks will respect your claim?' asked the Bruce.

'Well,' said the Red, 'you spent years being his lapdog, yet the revelation of our pact has left you without standing. Once you are out of the picture, the Scots will only look to me.'

He was already feeling quite smug and could not help gloating further so he faced the Bruce with a hateful grin.

'Farewell Robert. We led each other a merry dance, but it is now all over. Get yourself on the first ship to France or Norway, or to hell for all I care. Longshanks will show no mercy, he will have you torn limb from limb when his men find you.'

The redhead issued another mocking chuckle. He could not resist twisting the knife of betrayal, since he was filled with loathing for the Bruce. Yet as he readied to turn back towards the door, he found that his rival had already crept past him and stood waiting before it

'Let's settle this,' said the Bruce, 'once and for all.'

The Red took a step back as his rival drew his dagger.

'In a church? Have you not dug a deep enough hole for yourself man?'

'As you say John, I am left with no choice. I may only survive Longshanks' fury if I am the sole claimant. I may as well be dead if I do not leave this church alone.'

The Red suddenly realised that the Bruce was serious, so that he whipped out his own dagger and lunged forward, aiming it at his rival's breast. Yet the redhead's blade met with thin air, and dots appeared before his eyes as the Bruce's knee was buried into his stomach. The blow knocked the wind out of the Red, who fell onto the marble ground. He still held his dagger as he gasped for air, then groaned aloud when the tall figure of his enemy stepped towards him.

'Have you not backstabbed me enough for one lifetime Comyn?' cried the Bruce, the echo of his words as loud as a crashing rafter, 'confront me face to face for once!'

Although he was as versed in treachery as most men of his rank, the Red was no coward.

'Readily!' he cried, then rose onto his feet.

If he was to dance with death, he would first learn whether the Bruce fought with the dagger as well as he did with most other weapons. The two rivals moved warily along the edge of the faint ring of light, circling each other like rabid dogs ready to spring at the first sign of hesitation.

Outside the friary of Greyfriars, a band of men waited anxiously in the street.

'What can be keeping him so long?' mumbled de Kirkpatrick.

'Hope they're at least past the greetings,' groaned Lindsay, barely restraining a shiver of cold.

'Stay your tongues!' hissed a lord in their company.

Roger de Kirkpatrick and James Lindsay heeded the man's command, since he was Sir Christopher de Seton, the brother-in-law of their leader Robert the Bruce. Seton nodded towards another group of men who had appeared further along the road, and who served them with dark stares.

'They be the Red's folk,' whispered de Seton, 'I've met the fat one on the right. He's Sir Raibeart, Comyn's uncle.'

Both de Kirkpatrick and Lindsay said nothing, worried as they were about what was happening inside the chapel. They knew that the two lords' exchanges had been fiery at the best of times, with Comyn once grabbing the Bruce by the throat seven years earlier, at a Scottish baronial council held in Peebles.

'Hope they've not come to blows again,' muttered another man named Cuthbert.

'What? In a church?' said Christopher Seton, 'only a madman would do such a thing. It is why they met on holy ground.'

De Kirkpatrick sighed. Scotland had seen endless strife for years since King Alexander had died childless. This in turn led to years of succession disputes between the Bruces and the Comyns, who both had the best claims to succeed to the throne. Matters had deteriorated further because of the king of England, who had done all he could to weaken and take control of Scotland.

'Utter madness, this,' grunted Christopher de Seton nervously, as he loosened his sword in his scabbard and glared back at the Red Comyn's followers across the street. 'Utter madness.'

Although the Bruce was the taller of the two rivals, the Red by far preferred close combat. He waited until Robert tried to stab him, then spun sideways as his foe's knife edge missed his gullet by a handspan. The Red's swiftness filled him with a rush of daring, and he aimed a savage kick at his rival's crotch. A stunned grunt echoed against the walls as the Bruce collapsed to the ground, then rolled over sideways and tripped the onrushing John Comyn. The Red slashed at thin air with his blade, then crashed into the wooden benches along the wall.

Many months spent in the court of the English king had not softened the Bruce. He sprang back to his feet and dealt the rising Red a punch to the jaw which sent a tooth bouncing across the cold tiles. No sooner did the Lord of Badenoch's bloodied face hit the floor, than the Bruce hauled him back onto his feet and flung him towards the high altar.

As the Red crashed into the exalted table, the heavy statue of the crucifix behind it wobbled once before toppling onto the marble steps. The sound of its collapse was deafening, yet it still took a few moments for the Red to recover from his savage collision. When at last he stirred again, he turned onto his back and looked up at the Bruce who approached him like some growing nightmare.

'You would not dare,' gasped John Comyn, warily eyeing Robert's drawn dagger while he wiped fresh blood from his eyes, 'this is consecrated ground! Besides, I am the Guardian of Scotland, appointed by the king himself!'

The Bruce remained silent while his gait never faltered. Despite his dizziness, the Red somehow staggered back onto his feet, then seized a tall candlestick from the ground and flung it at his rival. The

Bruce dodged the iron missile with a slight dip of his shoulders, then raced at the redhead with a loud roar and smashed his forehead into his rival's face. The Red tumbled back to the ground with an agonised howl, then attempted a last stab at his enemy.

As the dagger tore through the air, the Bruce snatched up John's wrist and wrenched the blade out of his hand. Without a second thought, he next slammed it into the Red's chest. Blood appeared on the Lord of Badenoch's lip, while the Bruce's furious stare slowly turned into one of disbelief. He staggered away in shock, as the realisation of what he had just done cooled his rage like a pail of ice-cold water.

The Bruce almost missed his footing as he stumbled away towards the door. Meanwhile the mortally wounded Red seized the dagger in his breast, while his scream tore through the fleeing Bruce's ears like a malediction.

'Doomed!' he screeched, 'your lands forfeit! Longshanks will never stop searching for you!'

Robert turned to flee, and he had hardly reached the chapel door when a last cry reached his ears from the ravaged altar.

'The English will find you like they did Wallace!'

The fray was over, yet the Bruce felt suddenly overwhelmed by thoughts of Longshanks' terrible rage when word of the stabbing reached London. The door of Greyfriars chapel burst open as the Earl of Carrick ran into the street and fell onto his knees, staring at his bloodstained dagger hand. At the sight of their master, Christopher de Seton and the other followers of the Bruce pushed aside the gathering onlookers and made out the glint of tears upon Robert's cheeks. He shivered wildly as they helped him to his feet, when he cried aloud.

'I drew blood in a church!'

De Seton stared at him in horror.

'Did what?'

The Bruce stared at him, scarcely able to talk. De Seton looked over his shoulder and saw the Red's men drawing their arms. Then he met the Bruce's stare again and drew the mace at his belt, stepping back towards the gathering onlookers.

'Christopher...' said the Bruce in disbelief, yet his brother-in-law was already pushing his way through the crowd.

'Coward!' snarled Lindsay after the vanishing de Seton, as he grabbed the Bruce by the shoulder and hissed in his face.

'Did you stab the Red?'

'Yes.'

His portly follower swallowed hard in disbelief, before he finally managed a reply.

'Is he dead?'

'I don't know!' wailed the Bruce.

Lindsay swallowed hard and traded a look of dread with de Kirkpatrick.

'I'll make sure,' gasped de Kirkpatrick, then ran into the chapel with Lindsay close on his heels.

They had hardly run off when Comyn's men were seen running towards the Bruce, while the Red's uncle Sir Raibeart yelled at the top of his voice.

'John! John! What did you do to him, cur?!'

Cuthbert and two of the Bruce's remaining followers met the assault of the Red's men, yet not enough of the Bruce's men were left to fend off Sir Raibeart. The Red's uncle glared murderously at the bewildered Bruce, as he raised his sword in the air. He readied to split the Bruce's head open, while a man pushed the stunned bystanders aside. A crash of steel was heard when de Seton's first blow sent Sir Raibeart's helmet flying into the air. His second blow produced a sickening snap as the mace head cracked open the back of Raibeart's skull.

Comyn's uncle was dead before he collapsed to the ground, while Cuthbert's axe tore through the shoulder of one of the Red's men. Meanwhile de Seton drew his sword, using it to run through another enemy and then chase the remaining pair down the street. As they vanished around a street corner, de Seton made his way back towards Cuthbert and the Bruce. He panted heavily as he recovered his breath, while whispering beneath it all the while.

"Utter madness...utter madness..."

After they entered the chapel, de Kirkpatrick and Lindsay ran up to the high altar, where they turned the Red onto his back. They were left aghast by the gaping wound in his breast, and the Lord of Badenoch drew his last breaths as a trembling de Kirkpatrick lay the edge of his blade upon his throat.

'May the Almighty forgive me.'

The dagger was jerked sideways, shearing the Red's throat wide open. Hot blood was spattered everywhere, as Lindsay kicked John's hissing form back over. It was left abandoned before the ravaged high altar, which stood above a man whose treachery had all but made him the king of Scotland. When the blood spattered de Kirkpatrick ran back out into the street, he could see Cuthbert and Seton dragging a forlorn Bruce away with two other followers. The Red's uncle lay dead on the ground alongside other corpses, while Lindsay ran into the street with his blade drawn. De Seton was wholly winded from all the killing and spat on the ground.

'Let's get out of here,' he growled, as he noticed an English patrol at the end of the street.

The Bruce's followers needed no encouragement as they dragged their stunned leader towards a side alley. They entered it as the first light of the moon fell over Dumfries, casting the town in a deathly pallor.

Eight years later

Chapter I

STIRLING

Stirling Castle, 21st June 1314 AD

It just had to be Stirling.

The Bruce could still remember receiving word of Stirling Bridge almost twenty years earlier. The outnumbered Scots had defeated an English army at the bridge, so that William Wallace had inspired many, including the Bruce himself. At age twenty-three, the Bruce had ignored his family's appeals for reason and loyalty to Longshanks, the English king. For he had been filled with a patriotic fervor, instead taking up his sword and riding off to join the revolt against Longshanks. And while Wallace beat the English at Stirling Bridge, the Bruce joined other Scots lords to battle the English at Irvine. Yet the infighting between the Scottish lords was so great that they had been forced to surrender to the English troops led by Percy and Clifford.

Robert had been furious at the time, almost as angry as he felt riding up the steep hill towards Stirling, at the head of fifty men. He felt like chewing his whiskers in a blind rage, yet he had endured too much indignity and setback over the last seven years to be too easily overcome by emotion.

The Bruce had far more to worry about than indignity and setback. For since stabbing the Red at Dumfries, he had been declared an outlaw by the English and had also been excommunicated by the Pope. To make matters worse, following his coronation at Scone, he had been crushed by an English army led by the Earl of Pembroke. For more than a year, he had fled across the wilds of his own kingdom like a common outlaw, followed by an ever-dwindling band of men until he had been offered the protection of a powerful Isleman.

His family had borne the brunt of these setbacks, for his wife and daughter were prisoners of his enemies, with his sisters Mary and Christina held captive in wooden cages. Christina's husband Christopher de Seton, who had rescued the Bruce's life at Dumfries, had been captured by the English and torn apart within a year of the Red's death. As for the Bruce's younger brothers Nigel, Thomas and young Alexander: all of them had also been torn apart at Longshanks' order. Only Eideard, the Earl of Carrick, was still alive and free.

Would that Longshanks had torn him apart instead.

The Bruce instantly chided himself for the thought, since his brother had proven a staunch ally throughout the Bruce's slow but sure reconquest of Scotland during the last seven years. While the Scottish king reclaimed his kingdom castle by castle, Eideard had proven a fine military commander, even capturing castles like Rutherglen. Yet the Bruce could have wrung his younger brother's neck for entering a pact with Stirling's governor six months earlier.

The Governor of Stirling Castle, Philip Mowbray, knew that Eideard had not the patience for a lengthy siege. So Mowbray had promised to surrender Stirling to the Earl of Carrick if the English king did not relieve the fortress within a year. At the time Eideard's acceptance of the terms was considered chivalrous yet also shrewd, since the youthful King Edward II of England was distracted by a struggle with some of his barons. Yet even Longshanks's son was not fool enough to lose England's remaining toehold in Scotland so easily. So King Edward II had quickly and unexpectedly brokered a tenuous peace with his barons, while assembling a huge army which was marching on Scotland.

Hindsight was indeed a wonderful thing, and with hindsight Eideard's pact with Mowbray had been a mistake, something the Bruce was keen to try and rectify. The Scottish king rode atop a light grey palfrey, while he wore a golden circlet around his helmet as a sign of his exalted rank. His banner of the Rampant Lion was borne by his standard bearer, who rode in the front of the Bruce's mounted retinue of trusted comrades.

At the Scottish king's shoulder rode Angus Óg MacDonald, who was garbed in a saffron tunic and a leather jerkin. Angus was a high born member of the Bruce's men, for he was also the Lord of the Isles and chieftain of Clan MacDonald. He had granted refuge to the Bruce seven years earlier, after the English had tricked and crushed the newly crowned Scottish king at Methven. The Scottish king hoped that Angus and the other formidable members of his retinue might impress

Mowbray, although he could not be sure. For Mowbray had never once acknowledged the Bruce's kingship, while constantly refusing to surrender the castle to Eideard. The governor's pig-headedness and loyalty to the English crown was to be admired, particularly when one considered that the Bruce had practically reconquered the whole of Scotland during the previous seven years.

As the Scottish king's retinue made its way up the steep crag, the Bruce observed the high castle walls, as well as the roofs of the buildings behind them. Over the previous seven years the Bruce and his men had recaptured all keeps, yet Stirling Castle was truly impenetrable, perched as it was on such a forbidding height. The clop of hooves and the scrape of soles filled the esplanade when the Bruce and his men finally reached it, with yells and cries heard above the gate.

'It's the traitor, Robert Bruce!'

'Mad King Robin!' yelled another.

As archers fitted arrows to their bows, the Bruce reined his mount in a few feet away from the castle gate, then joined his men in cautiously raising his shield. The Scottish king did his best to look lordly and dignified, as a body of fierce-looking highlanders stood before him with raised shields. The Bruce quietly removed his feet from his stirrups, being ready to dive off his horse at the first sign of mischief.

'A warm welcome,' observed Angus at his shoulder.

'I've had worse,' replied the Bruce drily.

He had lost count of the times he had eluded capture and fought his way out of ambushes, following the disaster at Methven. Indeed had the Lord of the Isles not granted him refuge many years earlier, he doubted he would still be alive and standing before Stirling. The instants passed like long minutes until a stir was at last noticed among the castle guards. Philip Mowbray finally appeared atop the gate, his flushed face the picture of incredulity as he stared at the Bruce's party. At the governor's appearance, the Scots' standard bearer cleared his throat to make an announcement in as loud and haughty a voice as he could manage.

'His Royal Highness and King of Scotland, Robert Bruce, formerly Earl of Carrick, hereby declares to ye that he -'

'What's all this about?' roared Mowbray abruptly, cutting short the standard bearer's words.

The standard bearer appeared taken aback, staring at his king who spoke up in reply.

'You know why we're here, Philip. Cede the castle.'

The Governor's face turned a brighter red as he looked at his guards then back across the esplanade.

'Your brother would have told you that I shall not do it before the twenty-fourth of June. We entered a pact.'

'Your friends have broken their pacts with me before,' replied the Bruce.

'After you slew my nephew in a church!' snapped Mowbray.

The king of Scotland sighed. He could have argued that the Red had betrayed him to late Longshanks, but then Mowbray would probably go on to mention the many other grievances he held against the Bruce. Like the time the Black Douglas ambushed Mowbray and his thousand men on their way to Kyle. Mowbray had lost his sword during that conflict, and he had barely fled back to Bothwell castle with his life.

Indeed, thought the Scottish king, *the English chose the Governor of Stirling wisely.*

'I suppose,' said the Bruce, 'that it means nothing to you if the English find the whole of Scotland held by Scots?'

Mowbray snorted aloud.

'Spare me, Bruce. This is not about Scotland or England. This is about your own vanity and lust for power! Enough lust to even slay a man in a chapel? Madness!'

'You stand atop a castle gate not a pulpit, Mowbray!' yelled Angus MacDonald, the Lord of the Isles, 'so stop preaching. Just name your price and hand the castle over to its rightful king!'

'You mean a self-proclaimed king!' snorted Mowbray.

'No! I mean a king crowned at Scone and by a Macduff!'

'Aye a Macduff, who now lives in a cage like this usurper's sisters! All held prisoner for years, like his wife and child! Tell your friend to see sense, man! What you talk of is madness!'

'Mad King Robin!' yelled one of the guards again and Mowbray did not berate him.

At the Bruce's side, Angus MacDonald scowled at the Governor of Stirling Castle and yelled out to him.

'So you'll just hand over the castle to them like a meek, fawning lapdog?'

'What would you have me do? Claim your bribe to then find myself turning up at your door for refuge? After having my whole family killed or imprisoned?'

There followed a few moments of awkward silence, until Mowbray spoke again.

'Why are you really here, Bruce?'

The king said nothing for a few moments, while his retainers hung on his every word.

'Those colours atop your keep,' he said suddenly, 'are the king of England's colours. English colours atop a Scottish keep. The sight of them fills me with a deep resolve to keep up the fight.'

Mowbray mulled over the Bruce's words before he spoke again.

'Gallant words, Robert. You'll need all your gallantry when the English king rides up the Roman road. There'll be no more Highlanders' night raids or clever acts of stealth against thousands of England's finest. He has four times your cavalry and five times your footmen. I hear it is the largest army that England has ever assembled. Begone while still you can, you know how it always ends.'

The Bruce stared back at the governor who further pressed his argument.

'I've seen you from up here, training your men for months in the Torwood. That is all well and good. Yet what tactics would you employ against such sheer weight of numbers? Trap them on a bridge as Wallace once did? And do you really think that they'll fall for that again? You have no hope!'

One of Mowbray's retainers issued a cry of mocking laughter. Robert knew that the Governor spoke truth, yet he still stared back at him defiantly.

'So you will not surrender Stirling to your king?'

Mowbray snorted.

'Begone Bruce, I admire bravery but not lunacy. You should already be in Norway, seeking your sister's protection. Any day now, the English will reclaim these lands. And you know what they did to Wallace: a part of him was hung from these very walls! Not to mention your poor, foolish brothers. I admit you've been brave, yet your run of fortune ends here. I never bore much love for you, yet regardless I would still not do your bidding.'

So saying, Mowbray turned on his heel amid a swirl of finery, while yelling at his men to double their watch and keep up their spirits. When he was gone, the Bruce took in a last sight of England's colours, then spurred his horse which commenced its long canter back downhill. As he turned his back on the keep a loud farting sound was issued by one of the guards, yet the Bruce had suffered too much indignity over recent years to take any notice. As his party also began their descent, a last cry of insult was hurled at him from the walls. He had first heard it after his crowning at Scone, many years earlier, when even his queen had mockingly called him 'the summer king.'

'Mad King Robin!'

After descending Castle Hill, the Bruce's party rode back towards the New Park. The men did not trade any words as the wind picked up and Bruce's banner fluttered wildly. Then one of the MacDonald spearmen gestured in the distance. Between them and the distant sight of St Ninian's, they could make out a rider approaching them from across the meadow. The man's black hair swirled wildly in the breeze as the Bruce and his men instantly recognised him.

'Douglas,' said Angus.

Black Douglas' eyes always seemed to be ablaze while he wore his permanent smirk of contempt. MacDonald noted that Douglas' expression never seemed to change, regardless of the occasion. Yet the Bruce's best friend appeared more fatigued than usual, for his master had put him to work of late. For days James Douglas had busied himself with burning down every last barn and hovel that stood in the English army's path, even destroying the homes of countless Scottish tenants who had fled to the wilds. He had also been ordered to oversee preparations for battle while the Bruce rode off to Stirling. Douglas' smirk never wavered as he beheld the king's force, then tugged at his mount's reins and rode alongside the Bruce.

'They've reached Falkirk,' he said.

'Already?' replied the Bruce, visibly perturbed, then regained his composure and said 'lower your voice.'

As he kicked his steed ahead of the men after the Bruce and Douglas, Angus was as stunned as the king, for they had not expected such swift progress from Edward II's army.

'He must have marched them half to death,' hissed the Lord of the Isles.

'How many?' asked the Bruce, seeming suddenly paler.

'Hard to tell,' said Douglas, 'Keith sent a rider upon a blown horse. Said they could not even make out the baggage train from where he was standing. They saw the colours of Pembroke, Hereford, Gloucester, Percy, Surrey and the rest of them.'

'And Clifford too, no doubt.'

'Of course.'

They were all lofty lords who he had embarrassed during tournaments while he was still a respected member of Longshanks' court. All of them would have hated being beaten by a Scot, all of them would be keen to destroy him as they rode at the head of the massive English army. His spies confirmed Mowbray's warning, that the English had two thousand heavily armoured knights and 25,000 footmen.

An unbelievable number, thought the Bruce, *while my army is but 6000 men, which includes five hundred light cavalry. It is mad odds.*

He had ordered the leader of his cavalry, Marischal Keith, to ride south to find out if the numbers reported were true. The Scottish king sighed wearily as he rode through the large meadow and past a stretch of boggy ground to his left, which was called the Carse. It was caught between the two rivers of the Pelstream and the Bannock Burn. To his right stood St Ninian's church, in front of the forest of the New Park where his army was camped.

Beyond the forest he could make out the old Roman road. He knew that he would soon see knights riding upon it, haughty lords of the English king with their burnished steel armour and their pennons pricking the air. The Bruce thought of some of the nobles who Douglas had mentioned, of how he had once considered some of them friends while he still pranced around the court of Longshanks. One of whom had even saved his life by sending him sixpence and a pair of spurs.

Yet all shall cast friendship to the wind. All shall be desperate to claim my head as well as secure eternal glory.

'Marischal Keith may have learned more about their number,' said Douglas, 'he should return soon.'

'Mowbray confirmed their number,' replied the Bruce.

'Oh,' said Douglas.

'But not a word of it to the men,' snapped the Scottish king, 'and we must spread the word that they are disorganised and unruly.'

'Of a certainty,' replied Black Douglas.

'What of the pits?'

'Done.'

'Good. And the land scorched?'

'For miles around,' replied Douglas, with a hint of grim satisfaction, 'they'll not find a single chicken egg.'

The Bruce nodded his approval and for a while thereafter none of the three men spoke, for the size of the English army was still on their minds. Then Douglas spoke up again, mentioning tidings that the Bruce had hoped he would not utter.

'More men have turned up to join your army.'

'Send them away.'

'Can we not put them to some use?' replied Douglas, 'I doubt we've a quarter of Edward's force.'

'No,' said Robert, 'it is too late. We have no time to train them now. In days to come we cannot afford stragglers or lack of shape. They must be sent behind the Gilles Hill with the commoners, we will seek to train them later.'

'Yes, Your Highness.'

There was a hint of resignation in Douglas' voice, although the Bruce could not blame him for it. Yet there would be no protest from his men, who had followed him through thick and thin for the past seven years. Most knew that it was better to have a smaller, more mobile and organized force of handpicked men for the fierce fighting which lay ahead. Following Wallace's and his own setbacks, the Bruce knew better than to rely on men who were not committed to the cause.

He had also long given up on the cavalry support of nobles who had spoken empty promises and oaths.

His change in tactics had almost secured him the whole of Scotland, except for Stirling Castle. So he would do all he could to harry and hamper the English army until its spirit was broken. He might not have the numbers to meet them in the field, yet he was still one of the three greatest warriors in the known world, and still had time to devise more tactics to outwit his enemies. Despite the great odds that he faced, the Bruce was resolved to overcome his own despair. He would put on as brave a front as he could manage, so that his own troops, at least, might be fooled by it.

Chapter II

THE HOSTAGE

Rochester Castle, England, 21st June 1314 AD

The window in her quarters was her only comfort. They kept her in a small wing in the south-east tower of the quadrangular castle, where she often watched birds flying in the sky and the distant farmers. It was not a bad view afforded to her, for the keep was built upon a small rise near the River Medway. She could not believe how far she was from home, as far south as she had ever been before. There were many hours of silence and solitude, in which she wondered how she ended up a prisoner in the tower of an old keep built out of Kentish ragstone.

If all of her hate and loathing were the size of a keep, it would be a hundred times the size of Rochester castle, which had been her prison for almost fifteen weeks. She could still recall the day when she had been summoned from Barking Abbey, the fifth time that soldiers had appeared to escort her elsewhere. She remembered the keen sense of fear she had felt at their appearance, dreading the news that her husband had been taken captive or killed.

Sometimes she wondered why she felt so on edge, whenever she thought that she might receive news of her husband. Her marriage to him had been one of extreme, albeit brief, happiness, followed by years of horror and misery. In truth, news of his capture or passing would be the key that would finally liberate her from her gilded cell, yet deep down she still felt excited at the thought of him. She sometimes berated herself for her giddiness, recalling her mother's warning to always comport herself in the manner befitting of a lady, never to let her emotions take over.

Yet mention of Robert still provoked memories of his strength and ability at tournaments, in which he unhorsed one haughty knight after another. Which was not to mention his deft swordsmanship against celebrated opponents, with his every feint and parry being a testament to his hours of training. His martial prowess accorded him significant standing and popularity at court, where he was eyed as favourably by the ladies as he was by Longshanks, the English king.

This was all the more impressive when one considered that the Bruce had partaken of a Scottish rebellion against Longshanks in his youth. Yet after Longshanks had defeated Wallace, the Bruce's family encouraged Robert to submit to the English king. This had made him no less proud and haughty than the next highborn English lord, while being also possessed of a ready smile and a courtesy towards all men. Most of his peers envied him, yet many more were in awe of him, so that he was always surrounded by friends and admirers.

On her part, Elizabeth had been a nervous, young maiden only recently arrived in London with her retinue. The English had extended all courtesy to her, given her background. Yet her introduction at court had also met with keen stares from older men, few of whom were handsome, as well as the frosty, studious glares of other ladies in Longshanks' court. London had been an unsettling, confronting time, in which she did her best to be almost unnoticeable, which was not the reason she was at court. Her father's friends urged her to put herself forward and speak up more, which made her all the more nervous. So she felt almost liberated from all expectation when Robert laid eyes on her. At the time, she could hardly believe it.

'Lady de Burgh,' he had said, as he bowed and even kissed her hand.

He was already a renowned warrior despite his young age, who did not need to say much, except to serve her with a faint smile. She curtsied but returned his smile without ever blinking, so that the tongues of those gathered about them instantly began to wag, as they both knew they would. That the son of one of Scotland's two foremost families had approached the daughter of Ireland's most powerful man could never be a passing event.

Of course, in the tightly controlled world in which they lived, their mutual attraction alone would never have secured marriage. Nor would the Bruce have approached her in the way he did, if he had not deemed her a worthy mate. He had no doubt been instructed in womenfolk in the manner of men, with older warriors at times dragging their younger charges along, for a night of revelry and merriment in a drinking house filled with loose wenches. Yet a woman of her bearing would never be treated as such. For not even the king of England would touch her despite her being the wife of the Bruce, after Robert had slain the Red and claimed the Scottish crown.

In a world bound by strictures and rules, she had always found Robert liberating, in the way he took up arms and won his own honours. She knew he was a widower with a young daughter, Marjorie, yet this did not lessen his appeal. They were married shortly thereafter at his birthplace in Writtle, with her being a fresh-faced girl just turned eighteen and the Bruce twenty-eight. It had been a happy union, although she could not yet predict the horrors which would ensue four years later, after the Bruce was crowned king of Scotland at Scone.

Her recollections were interrupted by a knock on the door. It was time for confession. What she had to confess to, apart from being married to the Bruce, was beyond her. She was locked away all day like a bird in a cage, with only her embroidery and a daily walk with which to entertain herself. Apart from that, her only other pursuits were the constantly being summoned to hear mass in the morning and to engage in prayer.

'Hail, my lady,' came a timid voice at the door, 'I am here to hear your -'

'Yes, I know why you're here, Brother Matthew,' sighed Elizabeth. 'Please do come in. I am in dire need of some company.'

As she turned in her seat by the window, she could make out the wry smile of the young Matthew as he poked his head in from behind the door to her chamber and entered it. His brown cowl rippled about him as he awkwardly made his way towards a chair against the wall.

He pulled it out and placed it closer to her, a few respectful feet away. The young monk next engaged in a small bow before seating himself.

'So how are you, my lady?' he asked with a smile, albeit one which was not too broad.

Elizabeth silently took in the sight of the monk. He could not be twenty, she thought, far too young for a tonsure. He was handsome and would slightly redden whenever she passed him a compliment, perhaps betraying some ill-concealed feelings for her? In truth, Elizabeth yearned for the company of people other than servants and confessors, which had largely been denied to her during the last eight years of her being a hostage.

Yet she was grateful for the company of the bashful young Matthew, who was an improvement on her old, unfriendly confessor. The aged brother William, austere of bearing and with all the cheer of a granite slab, had recently passed away. She had barely ever spoken to him, but during her confession to young Matthew, Elizabeth never held back. She would sometimes mischievously make up a couple of impure thoughts which she had about men, only because it humoured her to see Matthew blush. Of late she had in truth missed riding horses more than she missed men, although that was curiously not even a venial sin. Elizabeth had sorely missed horse riding over the years, an activity which her custodians had always denied her. Stephen de Dene, the Constable of Rochester Castle, had also not considered her plea.

'And if you fall, and break your neck?' he had snapped at her, 'what should I tell the king then?'

After Elizabeth had made up and shared her latest confession, a still blushing Brother Matthew assigned her the usual penance of a few prayers and rose to leave the chamber.

'Please stay a while longer,' said Elizabeth, 'I am so lonely.'

Her confessor coughed nervously and sat down again.

'I suppose that a few minutes of chatter would not hurt anyone.'

'Thank you, Brother Matthew. I promise to say the prayers after you are gone.'

The young monk nodded with a hesitant smile, then looked awkwardly at the ground while making a feeble attempt at conversation.

'Do you want for anything?'

'No, thank you, Brother, just some company is all. What tidings from beyond this chamber?'

'Well,' he said, unsure whether to smile or be serious, 'I am sure you have heard of the king's impending foray.'

She nodded. One of her servants had told her that King Edward II of England had assembled a huge army and was marching north to destroy her husband. Matthew seemed unsure what to say, then upon noting her anxious expression he made a clumsy attempt to comfort her.

'You should soon be out of here, lady Elizabeth.'

She sighed aloud, so that he stiffened, wary that he might have distressed her. He made to speak up again, yet she cut in abruptly.

'It has been eight years since I last saw him,' she said. 'I have often reminded myself, whenever I dare to hope, that it was probably the last time.'

'Your husband?' said Matthew, then fell silent again as she quickly nodded to him.

'Yes,' she managed.

The young monk realised that she was upset and flustered, while thinking that it would be barbaric for him to rise and leave. It felt almost unchristian, abandoning her after she had opened up to him in that way. The hostage was locked away all the time, except for daily morning mass and an afternoon walk around the castle with two armed guards. There was nothing to lose in lending her an ear.

'Would you speak to me of him?' he asked softly.

She stared back at him, her face confused and doubtful for a few moments.

'Robert was not long crowned King of Scots at Scone,' she said at last, 'when the peasants already secretly mocked him for his audacity. They called him Mad King Robin and the King of Summer. I did myself tell him that we would only reign as king and queen of the May. A few months later, Robert was excommunicated by the Pope, while an English army marched north to crush him.'

'Was it the army that captured you?' asked Matthew gently.

'No,' said Elizabeth, 'for we were always travelling and desperate to elude them. Then Robert led us to Perth where Longshanks' lieutenant, the Earl of Pembroke, was stationed. My husband challenged the earl to battle, but they agreed to fight the following day, since night was setting in. Yet after we camped on high ground near the River Almond, Pembroke broke his word and instead attacked us at the dead of night.'

Brother Matthew's mouth fell open at this account, as he stared back disbelievingly at Elizabeth.

'That cannot be the truth, my lady. They say that Pembroke is an honourable man.'

'But it is what happened,' replied Elizabeth, 'we were taken unawares in our sleep.'

She could still remember Robert tearing himself away from her, the screams and tumult. Amid the deafening beat of hooves she had desperately tried to find Robert's daughter, the ten-year-old Marjorie. In the flickering torchlight she could make out the Bruce in his bedclothes throwing himself on a hobby before riding towards the mailed Pembroke and unhorsing Longshanks' man. It gained the Scots a brief respite, until the Bruce was himself unhorsed and sent flying to the ground. Elizabeth cleared her throat and resumed her account.

'Unknown to us, Longshanks had ordered Pembroke to deny mercy to my husband and all our followers. Robert formed a phalanx with Black Douglas and his subalterns. They managed to break us out, yet so many were slain. Robert ordered the Earl of Atholl and me to lead his sisters and daughter to Kildrummy Castle, held by his brother Nigel.'

'Ah, the Earl of Atholl,' said Brother Matthew, then refrained from saying anything else.

'No doubt you heard of his hanging in London,' said Elizabeth, 'before they burned his body and fixed his head on London Bridge. For at Kildrummy, we were captured by Scottish traitors and handed over to the furious English king. To our dismay, Longshanks ordered that we be separated, with Robert's sisters thrown in cages while little Marjorie was sent to the nunnery at Watton.'

Her confessor shifted uneasily in his seat, before sighing aloud.

'You have endured much,' he said.

'I am tortured by memories of that child,' admitted Elizabeth. 'To think she lost her mother at such a young age. I did what I could, yet now she has no one. I can only hope she is treated gently in the convent.'

It was a forlorn hope at best, given the girl's lineage, as they both well knew. The monk cleared his throat awkwardly as the hostage spoke again.

'In Yorkshire I complained of only having three clothes and no headgear or linen bedclothes. Yet I cannot imagine the torment endured by Robert's sisters or his daughter. I prayed for them when they moved me to Bisham Manor, Windsor castle, and the other places in which they have kept me hostage.'

She held her face to fight back the tears, while her confessor still beheld her in silence.

'It is not a happy state of affairs,' he said at last, 'yet her father is an excommunicated outlaw. What would you have the king do with the child? At least she is now safe from harm, committed to a life spent serving God.'

'You are speaking about my husband,' snapped Elizabeth, then fell silent while her confessor's jaw hung open.

'I am sorry,' she said at last.

Brother Matthew slowly rose to his feet and placed the chair against the wall. He thought he should leave her, yet he could see the fear in her eyes and did not wish her to be plagued by unease. So he stopped by the door of her chamber, looking at her over his shoulder.

'You do not hate me, do you Brother?' she asked suddenly.

'Indeed not, my lady. Why do you ask?'

'For being wed to England's greatest enemy, I mean.'

Brother Matthew sighed aloud at her reply.

'Surely you know me better than that, my lady. You see me garbed in the vestments of a monk, yet do not think I do not know how the world works. It is lordly men who rule it, you never had a choice but to be wed to the Bruce. Am I wrong?'

'No, you are right. I was drawn to him, but it was Longshanks who pressed for our union.'

Brother Matthew tarried in the doorway a bit longer, wondering if he should engage in further talk about the Bruce.

'You have my sympathy, my lady, truly you do. In the short time that I have known you, you have always exhibited good manners and grace. I cannot see the end of all things, nor have I walked in your shoes. So to me the Bruce will always remain a dangerous, excommunicated outlaw. Yet you must pray and believe in whatever you think is right and just.'

As the door creaked shut, Elizabeth was impressed by the young monk's wisdom which was beyond his years. She next slowly rose to her feet, feeling like a lonely, wretched creature as she made her way towards the window and stared outside it, wishing that she could see the distant, momentous events of the coming days unfold. Yet she chided herself for clinging to hope, for she had no part to play in those events.

'Which is not to mention,' she told herself, 'that everyone knows how it always goes when the king of England leads his army to Scotland.'

With a sigh she returned to her seat, then drew the beads from a fold in her cloak. She was tired of waiting and praying, waiting and praying. She might as well have been a cloistered nun rather than a highborn lady. Yet Elizabeth took some solace when she remembered Matthew's last words to her. So after taking a deep breath, she clutched her hands together and resorted to an act of absolute folly. For the first time in eight years she prayed not for her husband's soul but for his victory against the English king, no matter how implausible or unlikely.

Chapter III

THE PLOY

Falkirk, 21ˢᵗ June 1314 AD

How he missed Piers.

The English king could still remember first laying eyes upon the Gascon youth. He was smitten within an instant by the auburn ringlets of hair, which fell about a face rendered striking by thick eyebrows, high cheekbones and captivating full lips. Then there was the pair of light green eyes that seemed made only to gaze upon Longshanks' son. A striking pair of eyes; eyes that made young Edward feel like he was the only person that mattered in the world.

Which was not to mention Gaveston's haughty yet always appropriate manner with men of all ranks, his fearlessness and daring. The ladies often blushed at his very presence, women were known to turn into utter fools whenever he appeared. So that some of the men whispered envious mutterings about the foreign youth, quietly dismissing him as a dandy and a fop. Yet they were all made to eat their vile words when they crossed swords with him. For Piers Gaveston was both limber and strong, a man utterly devoted to swordsmanship who spent hours training and sharpening his martial skills. His father had provided him with the best teachers in Gascony, so that Piers had learned everything.

Gaveston was perfection.

As always, Edward fought back the prick of tears at the memory of Piers. He could recall the gentle touch and caring words, the soothing reassurances given to him by the Frenchman who had been like a brother to him. Although in truth, Edward knew that Piers had been more, much more, than just a brother to him.

He was a second son. Yet I bestowed every title on him, I would have given him more.

Longshanks had been an instant admirer of the young Gaveston's manners and skills, when he had turned up with his father in the court of the old English king. He was swiftly chosen to be a role model to the young prince Edward, who was instantly taken by him. They shared everything growing up, far more than Longshanks had first expected. Yet the wily, fearsome old king had soon picked up on the close relationship, being the first to ban Gaveston from his kingdom and his son's side. When Longshanks passed on, Edward had instantly recalled his favourite, only for twenty-one of his lords to become irritated by the Gascon's influence on their new king. They called themselves the Ordainers, with a few of their number banishing Gaveston twice more, before they took him captive.

And now he's gone. Against my own wishes. I was the king and could not protect him.

He could remember Piers screaming at him, urging him to act like his father and stamp out the lords' dissent. If only it was ever that easy. He needed the lords' support for the many battles his father had led the kingdom into. For Longshanks had always been involved in one war or another. If he wasn't putting the boot into the Welsh, he was off fighting the French. He'd also managed to fit in a crusade in his youth, when he'd even foiled an assassin's attempt on his own life during the dead of night. Which was not to mention all the trouble with the damn Scots. No matter how many times he crushed their rebellion, they were always up to trouble again once the king's back was turned.

Yet Edward had been appalled by the Ordainers' decision to take matters into their own hands and execute Piers. He had never seen that coming, news of Gaveston's death had destroyed him. Then to make matters worse, tidings had arrived from Sir Philip Mowbray, pleading for the king's intervention. The damned Bruce had besieged Stirling, so that Edward was forced to do the unthinkable and reconcile with lords like the Earl of Hereford who had put Piers to death.

Bastards. Bastards. But they shall pay, they shall all pay. I will see to it.

The king of England tried to ignore the summer heat as he leant sulkily against the neck of his muscular white gelding. Sitting up straight was too much of an effort for him, and he had little to no interest in the upcoming battle with the Scots. Its eventual outcome would be an easy victory for his exceedingly larger force of English troops, who were bivouacked alongside the Antonine Wall which passed through the town of Falkirk. His presence on the field was mostly symbolic, with the strategic details being left in the hands of highborn veterans like his lieutenant, the Earl of Pembroke.

Not that much strategy will be required. It will be yet another rout.

Pembroke had already defeated the Bruce several years earlier at Methven, in a deceitful manner which the young king still found admirable. His own father, the late Longshanks, had delighted in Pembroke's triumph for days after tidings of it had reached London. This act of deceit had taken place not long after Robert had been crowned King of Scotland, following his brutal killing of the Red Comyn at Dumfries. This outrage had led Longshanks to tear his tunic apart in rage before the Bruce was excommunicated by Pope Clement V in Rome. Longshanks had instantly ordered Pembroke to assemble a large force and ride with it to the north of England. Pembroke was also tasked with crushing the outlaws who had crowned the Bruce and assembled beneath his banner.

Which in turn meant that King Robert I of Scotland was left to face an English invasion shortly after his coronation. To make matters worse, the Scottish army was smaller than usual, for many Scots were still loyal to the Red's family and resented the Bruce. So, upon realizing that he might face heavy losses by besieging Perth, the Bruce put his own life at risk by challenging Pembroke to do battle on the open field.

On his part, the earl decided to exploit this challenge to his own gain, then declared that he would face the Bruce the following morning. Upon learning that their enemy had accepted, the Scots cheered, for King Robert was one of the most formidable warriors in the known world. To a man they felt assured of his triumph, so that the Scots readied for a good night's sleep and were soon all immersed in a deep slumber.

Many of them were barely roused from their blankets when the English cavalry led by Pembroke rode over them at the dead of night. Through this treacherous deed, Pembroke succeeded in annihilating most of the Bruce's loyal followers while losing less than a dozen horsemen in the process. The Bruce unhorsed Pembroke before fleeing into the woods with a few of his followers. His influence had been diminished for a very long time thereafter, yet the Scottish king had slowly but surely regained his power once more.

The Bruce would never be surprised again in his sleep, for he had in recent years survived so many attempts on his life by the English, that he would never fall for such a trick again. Yet Edward yearned to finish what his father Longshanks had started, and to wipe out the figurehead of Scottish resistance once and for all.

It would also silence the moaning of the dissatisfied and elderly members of the English court back home in London. They endlessly lamented that since Edward had inherited the throne from his warlike father Longshanks, England had practically lost all of its Scottish strongholds to the Bruce and his infamous lieutenants.

King Edward II was aware of the rumours flying across England, that he was a weaker and far less capable man than his father Longshanks, who throughout his life had shown little mercy to any vanquished enemy, no matter how valorous. Edward shook his head and banished the memories of his late father, since they made him feel weak and inadequate. It was not his fault that Robert had risen again and taken back so many of the English forts. It was the Ordainers' fault, for causing him so much distraction, all because of Gaveston.

In any case, once we crush the Scots on the battlefield, everyone will soon learn what a lack of mercy truly means.

Sir Humphrey de Bohun, Earl of Hereford, spurred his horse into a brisk canter as he rode from the council of war's pavilion towards his king. Other lesser lords rode after him, yet Edward instantly picked out the colours of his brother-in-law on the Constable's shield, with its argent stripe diagonally crossing an azure background with three golden rampant lions either side of it. At the sight of England's Constable, Edward was instantly overcome by a great hatred. For Sir Humphrey was also one of the Ordainers who had killed Gaveston.

On his part, Sir Humphrey felt the usual sense of revulsion as he approached his mounted sovereign. To him, Edward represented foppishness and folly. He scarcely resembled his late, fearsome father Longshanks, and Sir Humphrey groaned at the sight of the finely brushed curls twisted around his king's forehead, which pronounced the arrogant and pathetic stare of the pale grey eyes.

The Constable of England silently surmised that the war horse bearing his kingly brother-in-law held a higher air of authority and dignity than its rider ever would. Then he swiftly drew rein, checking his own horse's canter so that he faced his king. The thirty-year-old Edward raised his head and sullenly beheld his brother-in-law who was eight years his senior.

My, how he hates me. I'm not a patch on father in his eyes, nor will I ever be. I'll show him.

Edward broke the awkward silence, speaking in a high-pitched and whining tone of voice.

'I see that the discussions are ended.'

'Yes, my lord,' affirmed Sir Humphrey in his resonant voice, 'the rest of the council will be joining us shortly.'

'I see,' muttered the king of England, whilst rubbing one of the many valuable rings which adorned his hands. The moments passed by, but there was still no sign of the others.

This is a terrible bore. Best I talk to the old relic.

'What do the spies report on our formidable foes?' asked the English king, his voice possessed of a cutting sarcasm.

Sir Humphrey was renowned among other nobles because of his haughtiness and love of finery. Yet he suppressed a pang of revulsion at the youth's presumptuousness before replying.

'The usual,' he replied. 'The Scots are less than a third of our number and lack good weapons and armour. Their cavalry force is small, it numbers five hundred men. Their foot have trained for months in the woods, yet are made up of unruly Highlanders, unused to battles on the field. They may attempt to create schiltrons to fend us off with their pikes, yet we can cut them off or overwhelm them by sheer force of cavalry. Our archers will scatter them like sheep, just like your father's bowmen broke Wallace's squares here at Falkirk. Yet the men are exhausted. We should rest them today before pressing on to Stirling.'

Upon hearing this, the king of England looked bemused. He knew that the proud Sir Humphrey had an exceedingly low opinion of him, so he chose to embarrass his brother-in-law before the other lords present.

'I have absolutely no interest in your own petty conclusions, de Bohun!' he screeched, rudely interrupting Sir Humphrey, 'battle is not won by opinions but by superior strategy and tactics! Both of which, I am sure, will not be obtained from you!'

Edward paused to delight in the reddening of the older grandee's face, then continued.

'All I wanted to hear from you, Lord Constable, were our spies' reports. Your own views on how to engage with the Bruce's rabble are of no concern to me. Nor of any other worthy Englishman gathered here on this day!'

The king smirked as a few of the mounted nobles behind Sir Humphrey started to laugh. The public rebuking of England's distinguished Constable was something they had not witnessed before, so that they found the spectacle both unusual and funny. Meanwhile the blood had long risen to Sir Humphrey's head, which started to tremble slightly.

How dare this wench with balls instruct me in military tactics? And humiliate me in front of these lesser nobles! I should have remained behind with Lancaster, Warwick and Surrey.

Sir Humphrey rested a gauntleted hand upon his sword hilt, but at the last moment he succeeded in suppressing his murderous intentions out of loyalty to his wife and the memory of Longshanks.

'Your Majesty,' he finally managed, 'this is your first battle...I served your late father on many campaigns in the past...'

Edward was about to hurl more insults at Sir Humphrey, when more hoofbeats were suddenly heard in the distance, and both men turned to see three other knights galloping towards them. Among their number were the king's lieutenant in Scotland, the Earl of Pembroke, discernible by his blue and white striped shield which was chequered with red martlets. On Pembroke's left rode the Earl of Gloucester, with his shield sporting his house's gold crest with three red, inverted V-shaped chevronels. To Pembroke's right, bearing a gold and blue checked shield with a red stripe running across it, rode the Baron Clifford, Lord Warden of the Marches.

Edward observed the three approaching riders without feelings of animosity. For unlike Sir Humphrey, Pembroke and Clifford had always been loyal to him. The English king also trusted Gloucester, although the young Earl had indirectly caused the death of Piers when he had refused to help Pembroke rescue Gaveston from the Ordainers.

A young fool. Yet not a traitor like Sir Humphrey. I should have the popinjay strung up here and now.

As the men raised their visors and saluted their king, Clifford spoke up gruffly. He was the oldest amongst their number, a veteran soldier who had served Longshanks loyally for many years.

'Ah, Falkirk. Where your father crushed the rebel Wallace, Your Majesty.'

Edward acknowledged the remark with a slight nod of the head, when the young Gloucester spoke up heartily.

'And now to tear the Bruce limb from limb! And crush the damn Scots!'

'Hear! Hear!' snarled Clifford, as a grimace spread across his gnarled features which seemed hewn from old flint.

As a prince, Edward had always marvelled at the delight which the nobility took in oppressing those below them. After finding himself the head of an entire kingdom, he still could not understand the constant urge of the highborn to appear mighty.

But then father always said that a king should be feared.

He sighed aloud, feeling already bored by the days of drudgery ahead. As always, his army would ride deeper into Scotland and snuff out the rebellion, string up and kill soldiers with less means and armour. In truth a miserable, wretched business, yet one which always provoked such excitement among the nobility, who would be celebrated as heroes upon their return to England. It had always seemed such a dull exercise to Edward, to have to go through so much bother for so obvious an outcome.

At least the French put up a real fight.

Edward could not wait for the whole sordid business to be over; for the last two Bruce brothers, King Robert of Scotland and Eideard the Earl of Carrick, to be torn apart and their army crushed. So that he could finally return home and not worry about Scotland for a while to come. The place bored him so. It was such a bother to have to rally a whole army, to then listen to the bickering of angry barons for weeks thereafter, while they stamped out rebellion north of the border.

His father Longshanks had torn so many of the Scots apart, only for the flames of rebellion to grow all over again. This time he would see to it that they caused no bother anymore, although he was not yet sure what suffering he could inflict on them. For the natives vanished at the first sight of his army, and it was not as if he could torch a few villages and burn them to the ground. The Scots had already taken care of all that themselves.

'So has it been decided?' asked Pembroke, distracting the king from his thoughts.

'It has,' replied the king, 'it is why I summoned you.'

'Indeed, Your Majesty,' declared Sir Humphrey, having put his terse exchange with the king behind him, 'as the Constable of England I accept the charge to lead the army north. Yet we shall need leaders throughout the army to overcome the forces that the Bruce may -'

'Gloucester shall have command of the vanguard,' cut in the king drily, so that Sir Humphrey's words stuck in his throat while his lips still quivered and he turned a bright crimson.

'But Your Highness,' protested Sir Humphrey, hardly believing the dishonour which had just been cast upon him, 'I am the Constable of England and I -'

'And I am your king!' shrieked Edward, suddenly overcome by fury at Hereford's open questioning, 'and I say Gloucester shall lead!'

'But he is the youngest amongst us, sire,' said Sir Humphrey, undeterred.

Edward grimaced furiously for a few moments, while Sir Humphrey turned violet.

'I am your king,' he said at last, utterly exasperated, 'and I say Gloucester shall lead!'

'As Your Majesty commands!' declared Gloucester, while Clifford stared at the ground without betraying any sentiment.

Sir Humphrey beheld both men angrily then raised his voice again.

'We shall see about that!'

Edward was so enraged that he could not even talk, while Gloucester was also angered.

'The king has spoken!' yelled the young earl at Sir Humphrey, 'and you would do well to obey his order!'

'Or what?' growled the king's brother-in-law, 'will you leave your mother's teat and cross swords with me?'

'Such insolence!' cried Gloucester, 'have you not heard the king's order? This is insubordination, apologise at once!'

'I'll do no such thing!' roared Sir Humphrey, having tired of younger men serving him with orders.

Clifford looked downcast and Pembroke exhaled wearily and silently as he watched the king and the two earls squabbling among themselves. The lieutenant had had to put up with their quarreling all the way to Scotland.

A fop king, a popinjay Constable in Sir Humphrey and the inexperienced, slightly favoured peacock of Gloucester, mused the king's lieutenant, *not to mention the mad dog of Clifford, who at least only barks or bites when ordered to. Indeed, what could go wrong?*

'My lords!' roared Pembroke, after deciding that he had best divert the war council's attentions to a common foe.

One by one his fellows turned their attentions to him. The king, Sir Humphrey and the Earl of Gloucester were still shaking with rage, while Clifford's expression remained unchanged even though

Pembroke suspected that the warrior - who was oldest amongst their number - had also tired of the squabbling young fools.

'Regardless of who leads, my lords,' said Pembroke, 'we must attempt to lure out the Bruce. To lure the wolf out of his lair, to trick him. He is a hot-headed sort, perhaps we can avoid much loss of life if we play our cards right. Otherwise we'll be chasing shadows across Scotland while he constantly ambushes and slays our men.'

'What cards?' asked Edward, keen on anything which might hasten his return to London.

Pembroke was about to tell the king that his cross exchange with Sir Humphrey had given him an idea. For he recalled how the Bruce's lands had been given to the Constable's family following the murder of the Red at Dumfries. Indeed, the king's lieutenant had no doubt that the Bruce had little love for Sir Humphrey's house.

'We could have one of our finest challenge him to a duel. The Bruce is a chivalrous type, he might be tricked into it.'

'Who?' asked Edward with genuine curiosity.

Perhaps, thought the king, *the old snake might pull off another Methven.*

'The Bruce may have less love of Sir Humphrey or his house than you do, Your Highness,' replied Pembroke, 'the sight of anyone wearing the de Bohun colours should enrage him.'

'You want me to joust with the Bruce?' asked Sir Humphrey, wholly taken aback.

Pembroke could not resist a slight chuckle.

'What, and have you besmirch your fine surcoat with the blood of a usurper? Certainly not, Sir Humphrey. For I speak of your nephew.'

'Henry?' exclaimed most of those present at once, both startled and impressed by the suggestion.

'Who else?' asked Pembroke.

'I can have him summoned at once!' exclaimed Sir Humphrey, ''twould be a great honour for our house!'

Edward was not sure he wanted any honour bestowed on Sir Humphrey. Yet ridding himself of the Bruce without lengthy, filthy combat was somewhat appealing. Especially since he could do without losing men before his next battles in France. Furthermore, he'd not have to do any of the fighting himself.

Filthy fighting. Always hated it.

'Very well,' he said, 'fetch your nephew and get him to challenge the Bruce.'

Sir Humphrey's jaw was left hanging at the king's willingness to pursue the plan.

'At once, Your Majesty!' he cried, then wheeled his mount about and slammed his spurs into its sides, as he galloped off towards the camp.

'The rest of you, get some rest,' said Edward, 'we have tarried long enough in this place, and we'll be marching the men hard within the hour.'

As the lords took their leave, Edward turned away and studied the Antonine Wall, almost wishing that he could block the damn Scots out of his life with a wall, as the ancient Romans once did. Then he thought of Piers, and wondered what his late favourite would have made of the ploy to draw the Bruce into a duel.

Chapter IV

THE DUEL

The New Park, 23ʳᵈ June 1314 AD

At times Thomas Randolph dreamt of dying with a sword in his hand. He thought often about death, something he courted all too many times while fighting against and with Robert the Bruce. During these times of contemplation, Randolph assured himself that if he fought really hard and utterly wore himself out, then his death would be quick and painless. He could not have asked for more than a quick, painless death. After all, the lengthy executions he had witnessed after being captured by the English still haunted him.

Methven, he thought, *what a cursed day.*

He had been knighted by his uncle on the day of Robert's coronation. It had been a beautiful day, yet one also filled with an underlying sense of dread. For after Robert had slain Comyn in the church, everyone knew that it would only be a matter of time before Longshanꜰ would send an English army north.

Deep down Randolph knew that the Bruce had not been at fault. For the Red had betrayed his uncle's plans to Longshanks, so that it was only the secret warning of an English nobleman which had allowed the Bruce to flee from London unharmed. To next slay the Red had been folly, although it had rid the Bruce camp of their only genuine rival for the Scottish throne. The Bruce's supporters had of course claimed that he was acting in self-defence, albeit a bit too enthusiastically.

And then we got Methven.

Randolph could still remember it, days after the Bruce's coronation at Scone. Of the Scottish king treating with Pembroke, how they had agreed to lay down their arms until the following day, when they would be chivalrous and fight it out on the field. Yet Pembroke had broken his word and attacked the Bruce camp at night. As he stumbled over blankets, Randolph had seen the lady Elizabeth, his aunts and cousin attempting to get away. He had drawn his sword and hacked at the blurry shadows which attacked other blurry shadows, hitting out at anything that sounded like Englishmen.

Yet it had all been in vain. For he could also remember the heavy blow which had knocked him out cold. He opened his eyes later to find out - to his dismay - that he had not been killed, yet had instead been taken prisoner by the English. He remembered Pembroke who wholly ignored him, while Clifford and Deincourt laughed at him.

'Poor young fool Randolph,' they taunted, 'why did you stand and fight? And now Longshanks will have you torn apart.'

It was all he could do to face his eventual fate with bravery, to try to banish the thought of being hanged. In the following weeks he learned that the Bruce's own brother Nigel had been torn apart at Longshanks' order, following his capture. So Randolph had held little hope of being thrown in the dungeons, what with him being the Bruce's nephew. Then Adam de Gordon had unexpectedly interceded on his behalf, by personally guaranteeing that Randolph would not cause anymore bother. De Gordon also secured Randolph's peace with Longshanks within a year, when Randolph swore to the English king that he would be an enemy of the Bruce. He even chased down his uncle years later in the wilds of Galloway, getting so close to the outlawed Scottish king that Randolph even managed to seize the Bruce's lion standard and its bearer.

Then Black Douglas took me, he thought, *and I was spared yet again.*

The wily James Douglas had indeed captured him in a house on the Lyne-water, then led him to his uncle. Randolph had expected little mercy, as the Bruce addressed him severely.

'Nephew,' said the Scottish king, 'you have for a while renounced your faith, but now you must be reconciled to me.'

Yet Randolph was not one to break his oaths easily, so that he proceeded to openly berate his uncle for not submitting to the king of England. The Bruce sighed and ordered that Randolph be led to solitary confinement, left to kick his heels for days on end until he finally decided to take up his uncle's offer. The memory of these episodes often tormented Randolph. He sometimes wished that either the English or the Scots would have slain him, rather than allow him to keep changing sides. He could not understand how he had always been spared when so many others had been slain. Was it because he was not taken seriously? Was it because of the advantage that his intellect and bravery brought to a cause? Was it because he acted chivalrously at all times, until he was captured and forced by foul means to change allegiance again?

'Chivalry be damned,' he muttered to himself, 'it was chivalry caused bloody Methven, chivalry got me captured. Chivalry which has now led us into this mess.'

Randolph had heard of the huge army led by the late Longshanks' son, which was fast approaching Stirling Castle. King Edward II of England had driven his army half to death to reach and relieve the castle of Stirling. For months earlier, Eideard Bruce had unexpectedly made a compact with Stirling's governor, who agreed to surrender Stirling if the English king did not relieve the castle within a year. It had been a chivalrous yet foolish gesture, which had upset the Scottish king, and with good reason. For within a year, King Edward II of England had resolved his internal disputes with the Ordainers and assembled the huge army marching towards them.

'Chivalry again,' hissed Randolph angrily.

He sighed and pushed the warm body off him. There was a grunt and a low whistle, before she was sleeping again, as still as a log. He remembered the previous night, a night from heaven. The ringlets of hair on his shoulder, the gentle hands below his midriff, the limbs curled about him, the soft breath on his chest. She had put in a good effort and deserved the morning rest, yet Randolph watched her in the faint light of dawn with a prick of envy...

The previous day, at their king's orders, the Scots had gathered into four divisions led by the Bruce, his brother Eideard, Black Douglas and Randolph. They next picked up their pikes and formed square phalanxes, then marched towards where the edge of the wood met the Roman road, north of the Bannockburn. Their king had ridden atop a light grey palfrey, with a golden circlet around his helmet as a sign of his exalted rank.

When they reached the edge of the New Park, the divisions moved easily into position, having reconnoitered the ground many times before. Randolph instantly led his own squares towards St Ninian's Kirk to watch the track along the Carse, as had been agreed in previous days. Meanwhile the divisions of Black Douglas and Eideard occupied the stretch of Roman road between Randolph's and the king of Scotland's men. After posting sentries, most of the army readied to sleep while Eideard and Randolph shared memories over some ale, being unable to sleep.

Both men had received word that the English army was fast approaching, so that both agreed that – at least for one night - chivalry could hang. He had joined his uncle Eideard Bruce, the Earl of Carrick, to search for wenches. Together they rode behind the Gillies Hill, where the many camp followers and rejected soldiers were located. Most of them had been displaced from their homes by the Bruce's own men, since Robert had ordered his soldiers to burn anything which lay in the path of the approaching English army. Many of these people had grudgingly understood their king's motives, even offered their swords to fight for him against a much larger force. Yet he had sent them behind the Gillies hill to await further instructions, since Robert only wanted his schiltrons to be used in any ensuing conflict.

The Bruce's brother and nephew were riding through the bivouacs when a camp follower reached her hand out to Randolph. He had often rejected these advances, being largely unkeen to lie with the lowborn. Yet he knew it might be his last chance at union with woman, so he reached out his hand and hauled her up behind him.

'What's it like, to ride with a lord?' he couldn't help asking her, as she embraced him firmly and gently nibbled at his ear.

'Not sure, my lord,' she whispered, then proceeded to stroke his hair, 'I've never ridden a horse in my life.'

She had helped to numb the painful anxiety inside him, being as keen as he was awkward and uncertain. Yet Randolph banished all memory of their encounter, instantly reaching for his dagger when he heard the shuffle of footsteps through the canvas. Randolph surprised himself by the speed with which he drew his blade, he should not have felt so nervous within his uncle's own camp.

Then again, he thought to himself, *it sometimes feels like I've been on the run all my life.*

'Lord Thomas!'

It was the voice of his squire. Randolph sighed with relief and slid his blade back into its sheath.

'Gamelin? What do you want at this unearthly hour?'

'Yes, Lord Thomas. The king has summoned you. The English army has been sighted.'

'Shit,' replied Randolph.

His uncles Robert and Eideard would already be awake, as would bloody Black Douglas.

'Ready the hobby,' he snapped, as he shuffled over the blankets and searched for the clothes which he had hastily shed at night. After grabbing his doublet and hose, he stumbled out of the tent. A horse-boy led his mount by the bridle, while two others brought Randolph his armour. Meawhile Gamelin flicked his eyes at the tent and then stared at him askance.

'Give her a penny,' muttered Randolph.

'Are you sure?' asked Gamelin. 'Whatever happens this week, she can always say she lay with the king of Scotland's nephew.'

'And bear his bastard too, for her pains,' snapped Randolph, anxious about the English army. 'Just give her a penny, man!'

'At least you admit you're no prize,' muttered Gamelin, with a wry smile, as he took a coin out of his purse and flicked it inside the tent.

The squire next amused himself by the sight of Randolph struggling to pull his hose up from around his ankles. Despite his being a respected commander, Gamelin thought there was still something of the awkward scholar about Randolph, as well as something formidable. Randolph did not possess the brash aggression of the Bruce's brother Eideard, nor the wily cunning and ruthlessness of Black Douglas. Yet he knew that Randolph's stolid loyalty and learning appealed to the scholar in the Bruce, who was known for his love of learning and not just his prowess in battle. Not in vain did the Bruce hail Randolph as his most beloved nephew, despite his previous betrayal at swordpoint. In more peaceful times, Gamelin doubted that his lord Randolph would have ever drawn the sword, being better suited to a university or diplomacy.

Yet none of us decide the times we lived in, thought the old squire, *we can only do our best to survive what comes our way.*

It was Randolph's misfortune that he had been born in such tumultuous times, when the sword was needed more than the quill. And nothing, decided Gamelin, was likely to change in the foreseeable future. Internal squabbling and conflict with England was all the Scots had known for years, ever since the tragic death of King Alexander.

After swiftly attending to nature's call, Gamelin helped Randolph into his armour. They next proceeded towards the camp where the king had summoned his subalterns. As they drew closer to it, Randolph saw Eideard approaching with his retainers.

'How was she, nephew?' called the Earl of Carrick.

'Never you mind!' snapped Randolph awkwardly, while the younger Bruce laughed wickedly as they drew nearer to the Borestone.

Randolph could already make out the figure of his uncle flanked by Black Douglas and Marshal Keith, the aged leader of the Bruce's cavalry. Walter Stewart was also present, the young leader of a division of schiltrons which were in fact commanded by Black Douglas. At his approach some of the Bruce's officers eyed Randolph warily. It irritated him deeply, although he would have done the same in their place.

Such love and trust, after I retook Edinburgh. I might never be mentioned in the chronicles with Robert, Eideard or Douglas. But I shall still play my part.

The Bruce wore a hauberk and chausses as he stood before his men, with his standard bearing the rampant lion placed in the Borestone behind him. They were just over five thousand men at the edge of New Forest, all hand-picked and with a burning desire to die for their country. The king had trained them for weeks and weeks in the clearings of the nearby Torwood. Randolph had watched on in awe as his uncle's instructions were also heeded by the Highlanders from clans like MacDonald and Campbell, who formed the bulk of the Scottish infantry. For they were warriors that were used to years of wild charges and ambushes, yet at the Bruce's orders they held their positions in the schiltrons he had devised. Within weeks, the Scottish king had moulded his footmen into highly drilled squares of pikemen, that could employ both offensive and defensive maneuvers.

Yet apart from being a famous warrior, the king of Scotland was also a great lover of learning. His eyes widened and his voice rose while he held up some scrolls and read part of a poem named 'Battle of Maldon' to his men. It was an inspiring account and also timely, for it recounted how a small Viking force had defeated a much larger English army.

There was a harsh meeting.
They stood fast, warriors in conflict.
Warriors fell, weary with wounds.
The slain fell on earth.

Oswold and Eadwold all the while,
both those brothers, strengthened the men,

with words bade their kin-friends that they should endure at need,
unweakly use weapons.

Byrhtwold spoke, raised his shield
– he was an old retainer – shook his ash-spear;
full boldly he taught warriors:

"Thought must be the harder, heart be the keener,
mind must be the greater, while our strength lessens.
Here lies our prince all hewn, good one on grit.
He may always mourn who from this war-play thinks now to turn."

When the king finished reading in his deep voice, he beheld his men with a wide grin and stood aside to let the abbot of Inchaffray deliver mass. After it was heard the Scots prayed to God for their cause, observing the vigil of Saint John the Baptist by only eating bread and water afterwards.

As the men proceeded to form their squares, a messenger was sent by the king to each division, urging any that were faint of heart to depart at once. Yet all Scots declared that they would conquer or die. Meanwhile Randolph dismounted and handed his horse's reins to his squire.

'Lead it off somewhere safe, Gamelin,' said Randolph, 'I'd rather form part of the schiltron.'

So saying, he stepped among the five hundred men in his division, who hailed from his earldom of Moray and from Ross. They also included the burghers from the towns of Inverness, Elgin, Nairn and Forres. Each of them rested upon their pikes while in the distance they could make out the Bruce and his other lieutenants barking orders at the men who fell into their assigned positions. Hours passed before a cry went up alongside the Roman road, where the Bruce's division was posted. In the distance, numerous colourful pennons and lances could be seen pricking the air south of the Bannockburn stream, along with the shining helmets worn by an infinite number of English knights.

'Withdraw!' yelled the Bruce at his officers, as the advance of the enemy across the meadow slowed as they crossed the Bannockburn stream and returned onto the Roman road.

Gamelin sought out his lord as the English knights drew nearer.

'Hereford's colours,' said Randolph, as he made out the blue and white standard of the Constable of England, which was spangled with golden lions.

'So many horsemen,' replied his squire, yet Randolph was surprised when a solitary knight came into view, some fifty yards ahead of the main cavalry. He wore shining armour and brandished a long, striped lance. His shield bore the colours of Sir Humphrey's house, and he reined his mount to a halt when he was just within bowshot of the Bruce's men.

'Shall I pick him off, Sire?' called Nevin, captain of the Scottish archers, as he raised his longbow.

'No,' said the king of Scotland, 'let's first hear what he has to say.'

The knight ahead of them raised his visor, revealing young and fair boyish features.

'Why behold that lad,' exclaimed Angus Óg, 'looks like he's been torn from his mother's bosom!'

'Looks can be deceiving,' remarked the Scottish king drily.

'Robert the Bruce!' cried the young Henry de Bohun, 'will you who calls yourself king of Scotland face an English knight in single combat?!'

His sharp voice resounded across the meadow like the crack of a whip. The Bruce already knew of the knight's reputation, having heard that the young de Bohun was an as yet undefeated champion at Edward's tournaments. He also knew that many years earlier, Longshanks had given the Bruces' castle of Lochmaben to the de Bohuns. His knuckles whitened about his battle-axe, while his brother Eideard swiftly abandoned his division and rode hard towards the Bruce.

'Don't do it, brother!' yelled the Earl of Carrick, 'let me go instead - they won't tell the difference!'

The king of Scotland sighed.

'And if you die, what then?' he asked, 'would you want my people to take me for a coward?'

Eideard struggled to speak for a few moments.

'Would you so readily risk all you've accomplished?' he muttered.

The Bruce nodded at his brother and looked once at his men, then spurred his horse down the slope with a kick of his heels. The Abbot of Inchaffray made the sign of the cross and mouthed a silent prayer as the Bruce bore down upon de Bohun. The gathered Scots stared on at the upcoming clash in fear, knowing that their future was bound to that of their king. Near the Bannockburn, both Sir Humphrey and Gloucester grinned as they watched the two combatants galloping towards each other in full view of both armies.

The wind ripped through Robert's shaggy hair as he bore down full tilt on de Bohun. Yet the Bruce was no longer the rash and hot-headed lord from his youth. Years of suffering had rendered him rawboned and wily, so that it was a scarred, hardened warrior who descended upon the English champion like a bird of prey. He knew that he could demoralise the entire host of invaders if he timed everything right. Yet his hatred for the de Bohuns seethed in his blood and he was already panting heavily like a raging bull.

On his part, Sir Henry thought he could not have faced a better rival. For as he pulled down his visor and thundered towards the Scottish king, he soon realised that descending upon him was a rider without lance or shield, whose charge was so swift that de Bohun would simply have to aim his lance at the man's chest. The distance between them was swiftly reduced with the two combatants soon only yards away from each other. De Bohun shuddered uneasily when he caught sight of his enemy's flaming eyes and gritted teeth, then regained his nerve and lowered the tip of his weapon towards the Bruce's ribs. It was all too easy.

Just as Sir Henry's lance was about to run him through, the Bruce rose in his stirrups and leant slightly to his left. With a sudden jerk of reins he had his nimble mount skip sideways, so that the point of de Bohun's lance missed the Scottish king by a hair's breadth, slicing open the side of his leather jerkin and glancing his armpit. The Bruce's limbs felt ablaze as he rose in his spurs and brought his axe down upon the head of Sir Henry, who had lost a mounted duel for the first and last time in his life.

The blow tore the steel helmet apart like sackcloth, and from within it there was issued a burst of blood and brain which spattered the king's arm. De Bohun wobbled once as his horse charged on, then toppled out of his saddle. The duel was over as soon as it had begun.

Chapter V

RANDOLPH'S REDEMPTION

The New Park, 23rd June 1314 AD

The cheers from the Scots were already deafening. As the English knights looked on in horror, the king of Scotland wheeled his palfrey about and rode back towards his men. Randolph beheld his uncle in disbelief, for he could hardly believe the daring and skill he had just witnessed. Gamelin was roaring at his shoulder, taking up the cry which spread through the divisions of Scots like wildfire.

'I can't believe it,' said the king's nephew, then groaned when he saw English knights charging towards the Bruce, who was but a few feet away from his schiltrons.

'They attack!' cried Gamelin.

Meanwhile Angus *Óg* could be heard yelling at the Bruce as the Scottish king reached his men.

'Are you mad? Why risk your life like that?'

The Bruce looked at his broken axe handle and sighed.

'Now also my axe. I've lost too much in this war to the English.'

Then he flung it away and dismounted, for already he could hear the great pounding of hooves on the Roman road as the charging cavalry made its way towards his footmen.

'Withdraw!' he yelled, as the cry was taken up by his officers.

The schiltrons took a few steps back towards the wood, in an attempt to further embolden the invaders. The ruse instantly worked as Sir Humphrey could be heard yelling at his fellow knights, urging them to ride harder.

'They fly to the woods! Cut them down!'

The ground shook as the Bruce suddenly raised his arm, instantly ending his division's retreat.

'Hold!' he yelled, as his men took up their posts and seized up their pikestaffs.

The men at the front were already leaning forward on one knee, while their fellows behind them stood with legs apart and readied for the ensuing impact.

'Hold!' cried the Bruce, waiting until the onrushing force grew larger, then bellowed his final command.

'Draw pikes! Forward!'

His squares of men held out their lengthy spears, resembling a bristling hedgehog as they leant forward in unison towards the English. Sir Humphrey groaned as his men crashed into the Scots' raised blades amid the snapping of lances and the screeching of skewered mounts. Having withstood the cavalry charge, the pikemen drew their blades and fell upon the fallen horsemen, shoving their dagger points through gaps in the armour. It had been an almighty impact, yet the Bruce was already screaming for his men to close ranks, to take the place of those pikemen who were wounded or stunned. His men instantly took up his command, for they had been drilled for weeks on end.

Sir Humphrey's remaining knights chose to fan out when they witnessed the fate of their skewered comrades. Yet as they led their mounts off the Roman road to encircle the Scots, their horses fell into the many low wolf pits which the Bruce's men had dug up during the previous nights. Amid the whinnies and howls of despair, these unfortunates were in turn spotted by Gloucester and his knights who watched the setback unfold from across the Bannockburn in sheer disbelief. They circled back and attempted to cross the Bannockburn further upstream. Yet they were instantly spotted by the Bruce's brother Eideard.

'Forward!' cried Eideard, with his divisions of pikemen instantly marching in orderly formation towards Gloucester's riders, ready to skewer them with their pikes held at the ready.

No sooner did Gloucester see the approaching divisions of Eideard, than the young Earl reined in his horse, suddenly wary of the other traps laid by the Bruce. At his unexpected gesture, his charger missed its footing, sending Gloucester tumbling to the grass. The young nobleman issued a barrage of curses as he returned to his feet, then hurried to mount his horse again. Behind him his knights slowed to a canter as they awaited the earl's next movements.

'Zounds!' cursed Gloucester aloud, then clambered atop his mount and rode back towards the English army, with his knights following close behind.

'They flee!' yelled Eideard, with his men cheering aloud mockingly and shaking their fists at the backs of their highborn enemies. Meanwhile the Bruce's men were cutting down the last of Sir Humphrey's knights who had not yet withdrawn with their master.

The Bruce's brother stood in his stirrups and cheered as he rode towards the Scottish king's men, punching the air and crying out loudly.

'We have bloodied their nose!'

Yet when he drew nearer he could see that the Bruce was staring aghast beyond him and towards a distant pass, where a body of at least three hundred horsemen thundered towards the city of Stirling. The Scottish king spurred his palfrey forward and rode with Eideard towards the men of Randolph.

Randolph was still slapping Gamelin's back when he made out his two uncles approaching on horseback, closely followed by their other retainers.

'Most beloved nephew!' yelled the Bruce, 'a rose has fallen from thy chaplet!'

Randolph was horrified by these words as he looked up and made out the distant banners of Clifford and Beaumont, as the knights thundered towards Stirling.

'Christ's nails!' he gasped, then yelled at his men to advance.

At his command, his men seized up their pikes and marched towards the meadow, slowly but in step. Yet within moments, Randolph loudly urged his men to increase their pace, for he could see that Clifford's colours were getting ever closer to Stirling, and could also encircle the Scots' left flank. As his men rushed out of the woods, their shoulders met as they formed an impenetrable wall of spears.

Randolph's men were barely halfway towards the English knights when Clifford could be seen wheeling his steed around towards them. As his knights followed suit, Randolph instantly called for a halt, his voice straining to reach above the distant thundering of hooves. As his men took up their posts, Randolph knew that they had no woods to protect their back, so he called for the circular formation.

'Are you sure, Tam?' asked Gamelin, 'they did not work at Falkirk.'

'Yes,' said Randolph, 'for they have no archers.'

Two circular and impenetrable hedgerows of stakes were swiftly created, as the contingent of knights drew ever nearer. As he charged towards the Scots, Clifford laughed aloud when he noticed Randolph standing amongst his men.

'Traitor!' he cried, 'today you shall pay for your treachery!'

Yet the Scots' pikes snapped forward in unison, so that it was all Clifford could do to veer away from them, with a pike end glancing his mailed shoulder as the other English knights like Beaumont and Deincourt also galloped around the pikemen. Meanwhile Randolph roared at his footmen to bunch tightly together and to keep their shape. Every now and then the English knights attempted to break through the circle of spears, yet it was no use, with sharp steel often passing through a horse's breast or a knight's neck.

'Damn them!' roared Clifford, 'damn them to hell and back!'

In his frustration he hurled a spear and also his mace at the Scots below, with his action soon taken up by his furious fellow riders, some of whom also hurled their axes and swords at the Scots below them. Yet most of these weapons clattered harmlessly off the wooden pike ends, with the Bruce's men ever ready to lunge forward and catch a horse or rider in either throat or chest. As the hooves pounded the grass, a great haze of dislodged turf rose in the air, so that it soon seemed like Randolph's men were trapped in a swirling, rising cloud which masked them from view.

Among the trees the Black Douglas observed proceedings below him, somewhat concerned by the great force of horsemen which surrounded Randolph's men.

'Christ's blood,' he snarled, causing the newly knighted young Walter Stewart to pale at the imprecation, 'Randolph will never get out of there.'

So saying, he spurred his mount south towards the divisions of Carrick and his king, finding the Bruce brothers mounted alongside each other as they also observed Randolph's fighting from afar.

'Rab!' yelled Douglas, 'I must go to his aid!'

'No,' replied the Bruce, 'do not abandon your post. The English might renew their raid on us.'

'So we leave Randolph to be torn apart!' replied Douglas, for he was perhaps the only person in Scotland who could openly question the Bruce.

'No,' repeated the Bruce, 'you simply leave him be, for now.'

Across the meadow, Randolph beheld the charging knights nervously as their gallop around the pikes continued. He attempted to shield his eyes from the glare of the sun, as sweat ran down his neck and sides.

'I cannot make them out,' he muttered to Gamelin, 'so many and penning us in.'

Gamelin said nothing as he stood with his sword drawn alongside the Bruce's nephew.

'Let them ride,' he muttered, 'so long as our pikes are out they can never come close.'

Then a cry from one of the pikemen was heard at their back, as a caparisoned stallion came crashing towards the wall of spears and hurled itself screeching at the men. Scots were knocked unconscious as a half dozen spear ends passed through the mount, with its rider hurling himself off its back and colliding into the stunned Earl of Moray. Randolph's sword was struck from his hand as the hefty form of Sir William Deincourt pinned him to the ground. The same knight who had jeered him after Methven drew his sword from his side, then shoved the point against Randolph's breast, which caused the Bruce's nephew to issue an agonised cry.

'Traitor!' growled Deincourt, frustrated by the steel rings in Randolph's hauberk.

Sir William had been loathe to lose his horse, yet he had thought the price worthwhile, if only to rid the schiltron of its leader. Deincourt also knew that the loss of the Bruce's nephew would be a significant blow to the king's morale. Meanwhile spots danced before Randolph's eyes as he sought to ignore the pain of the sword point in his breast. He tried to wriggle free from beneath the old Sir William, yet the English knight's heavily armoured body pinned him down, while the sword point bit deeper into the mail along his chest.

'Tam!' cried Gamelin, rising off the ground as Deincourt rose above Randolph and withdrew his sword, lifting its point briefly above the Earl of Moray's face.

Then Randolph's hand fell upon a mace on the ground, which had been flung at the Scots by one of Clifford's men. Sir William's sword point was already descending when the blow of Randolph's weapon to the side of the English knight's head caused a shower of teeth to be knocked out of his mouth. Deincourt's head jerked unnaturally leftwards and he fell dead at Randolph's side. The Earl of Moray pushed Deincourt's corpse away and was helped back onto his feet by the shocked Gamelin.

'Tam!' cried his squire, 'are you hurt?'

'Barely scratched,' he gasped, then howled at his men to hold their positions.

'Christ's blood,' said Douglas, as he beheld Deincourt's attack, followed by the attempts of other knights trying to break through the schiltron, 'we can wait no longer.'

He galloped over towards the Bruce again, with the king beholding him in surprise while he yelled.

'Surely it is the only attack, Rab!'

'Go then!' replied the Bruce, for he was also concerned that Randolph's force might be overwhelmed by the sheer weight of riders which still encircled them.

Douglas made back to his men, cupping a hand around his mouth and calling out to Walter Stewart.

'Onwards, Sir Walter, to aid Randolph forthwith!'

Upon hearing this the young Stewart instantly ordered his pike-men to enter the fray, with Douglas catching up with them just as they left the cover of the woods. As they made towards Randolph's men, some of the English knights wheeled about and charged towards them.

'What's that?' asked Gamelin, as he stood besides Randolph while the pikemen still held the enemy at bay, 'Black Douglas has finally grown a heart?'

Randolph looked on in wonder as half of Clifford's riders broke away from his schiltrons to charge the men of Douglas. This instantly eased the pressure on the Earl of Moray's men, yet he thought he could do one better and break the cavalry formation which still assaulted him.

'Order them to regroup,' he gasped at Gamelin, 'to resume the usual formation. We attack.'

'Attack?' exclaimed his squire, 'have you taken leave of your wits?'

'Long ago,' replied Randolph, 'now give the order.'

At his squire's cries the circle formations were abandoned as the schiltrons resumed their square, phalanx shapes. When this was ac-complished, Randolph yelled at the footmen to advance, so that the pikes were suddenly and unexpectedly used to attack. The surprised English knights were split in two, leaving them disjointed and scat-tered. Many a knight fell to the ground after receiving a cruel pike end through the throat, until Clifford's strident voice could finally be heard rising above the cries and angry shouting.

'Retreat!'

One by one the knights wheeled away and thundered back towards the English army, hot on the heels of Clifford who had already bolted away with a few loyal retainers.

'Victory again!' cried Gamelin in disbelief, while behind him Randolph fell to one knee out of sheer exhaustion.

Chapter VI

THE VISITORS

Rochester Castle, England, 23rd June 1314 AD

Lady de Burgh's heart leapt when she heard the afternoon knock on the door. She was already seated and waiting to make her confession, although she was more interested in the company. However much she relished her afternoon walk in the castle courtyard, she found that the frosty looks which she received from her silent armed guards did not do much to lift her spirits. So Elizabeth was already smiling when she made out the timid, handsome face of the monk as he passed through her door. Matthew smiled back at her half-apologetically.

'Do you need to confess?' he asked sheepishly.

'I thought you'd never ask,' she replied, then issued a low chuckle.

During the sacrament, she could not but tell him that she had erred by clinging to hope for her husband's victory, no matter how unlikely.

'Yet for an excommunicated outlaw to prevail,' he whispered, 'would that not bring discord and treachery to prevail across the land?'

She had not replied, resigning herself instead to reciting the prayers which he had assigned to her as penance. With typical courtesy, the young monk patiently waited alongside her until she was finished. They next spoke about Matthew's background, since they had over previous encounters long exhausted the subject of her life and misfortunes. So that the Lady de Burgh learned that he hailed from the nearby village of Boxley, which was not two leagues distant from the castle. He also told her that his old, widowed father was a blacksmith who still toiled at the anvil, with his three brothers having marched north with King Edward II to fight her husband.

'Father is proud of them,' he said, 'they have always done him proud.'

'Is he not proud of you?' she asked.

Matthew stared back at her, seeming uncertain what to say.

'I don't know. They always saw me as different. I was quieter and more timid. I had a mind for letters, it did not go unnoticed by our parish priest. My mother, bless her soul, encouraged me to pursue the path of the Lord. Father would have preferred me to help in the smithy, yet she urged him to respect the summons of the order.'

'Was she at least proud of you?'

'Yes, I believe so,' he replied, 'although news of her passing reached me while I was at the college.'

'I am sorry,' said Elizabeth.

'Alas, my lady,' he replied with a faint smile, 'such is life.'

Great whinnies were suddenly heard outside, which were followed by the unmistakeable creak of the castle gate. Elizabeth and Matthew beheld each other in surprise and rose to their feet, quickly hurrying towards the window. In silence they made out a man wearing a pointed cowl attached to a robe which stretched over his shoulders, as he thundered over Rochester bridge towards the keep. A half dozen armed riders rode after him, and as he entered the courtyard he was greeted by Stephen de Dene, the Constable of Rochester Castle.

'He looks like a diplomat,' said Elizabeth in surprise, then added: 'from London.'

Matthew said nothing as he stood alongside her. He was surprised to feel nervous that these men might have appeared to take lady de Burgh away.

'I recognise him,' she said suddenly, 'I remember that face from the king's court. He is John Bigod, a distant relation of the Despensers.'

Her confessor nodded and said nothing, for the very mention of the notorious Despensers flooded him with unease. They were notorious for their political maneuverings and criminality, which had led to much upset and tumult across the land.

In truth, thought Matthew, *it was just as well that trouble with the Bruce broke out north of the border. It forced us English to stop fighting one another and to make peace.*

'Let us be seated again,' said Elizabeth after a while, when the men vanished from view. 'Would you like refreshment? The Constable's wife recently sent me some wine from Vinesfield.'

'Some water, perhaps,' replied Matthew as they returned to their seats, which prompted Elizabeth to pull out and ring a small bell.

Yet no servant appeared at the door, which was heftily swung open by Constable de Dene himself, who cast a fine figure in his damask surcoat. He was closely followed by the recently arrived John Bigod and two armed men. At the sight of her custodian and the visitor, Elizabeth quickly rose to her feet and bowed her head down low, while at her side Matthew did the same. Yet the Benedictine monk may as well have been invisible, since he did not earn a single sideways glance from the new entrants.

'Lady Elizabeth,' said de Dene, yet he did not bow to her, since she was a hostage and disgraced by her marriage to the Bruce.

'My lord,' said Elizabeth, with a low curtsy, 'to what do I owe the pleasure of your –'

'This is John Bigod,' cut in the Constable, interrupting her and stepping aside, 'he is arrived from London to give you good news.'

For a few moments Elizabeth could not speak, for she suddenly feared the worst.

Robert...is he dead?

'My lady,' said Bigod, never taking a step towards her and staring at her feet, 'your captivity is soon to be ended. I have been sent to bid you to prepare to leave this place and return with me to London. Your unfortunate union with the outlaw Robert Bruce will soon be ended. Your father has arranged for you to return to court, you have many suitors waiting in the wings.'

After the diplomat had spoken no one said anything, until the Lady de Burgh finally managed a reply.

'But I am already wed.'

'For now,' agreed Bigod. 'A most unfortunate business, yet not one of your own volition. Also one which has cost you many years of freedom. Yet you should take heart, for you shall soon be free again.'

'So Robert,' she managed, 'I mean my husband, he is not yet -'

'Not yet,' cut in the king's man, 'although it can only be a matter of time now. The king is abroad and will soon attend to that. Now you must prepare yourself to depart Rochester. The Constable's Christian hospitality towards you has been exemplary, and should -'

'I will do no such thing,' was the woman's terse reply.

'Your pardon?' said her custodian de Dene, with his face turning red while his jaw hung open.

'The arrogance of your demands,' she snapped, suddenly finding an unexpected strength within her. 'My husband, regardless of his status, is still alive. Did you promise the jailed wives of English rebels to others before their husbands were captured and punished? This is a disgrace, I'll have no part in it.'

She was surprised when Matthew piped up behind her.

'I-I am afraid,' he managed, 'that the lady speaks truth.'

'Stay out of this priest!' roared de Dene, 'do you know who I am? I will have you banished from this land and stripped of the priesthood! This woman is fortunate to still be considered eligible for holy matrimony, after her bond to such a treasonous butcher. She should be on her knees and kissing our hands, for aiding her to obtain freedom and respect once more.'

'It is you that denied it to me,' she replied tersely.

The men's arrogance had got her blood, and she would not be spoken down to.

'Lady de Burgh!' cut in John Bigod, 'you must act now before your stock further diminishes! Once the Bruce is captured and killed, you will be the widow of a traitor! There is no other path for you but to regain your honour while you still can!'

'A traitor,' she whispered, staring at the ground and trying to regain her composure, 'a traitor you say? Did Longshanks push me into the arms of a traitor?'

'Have a care for your words, my lady!' growled de Dene, 'do not mock our late king!'

She clenched her fists and looked away.

'I need time to think.'

'There is none!' cried Bigod, 'let us hasten you away to London, where you may start life anew!'

Her mind was in a whirl at their insistence, she could not think properly. Deep down her conscience nagged at her. For she had often thought that if Robert was captured and killed, it would release her from her daily hell. Then she remembered his courage and fire, she knew he had not chosen her idly. She was the daughter of a de Burgh, she would not be spoken down to by these mere vassals.

'Come now, my lady,' said de Dene, 'let us help you to prepare your belongings and aid you to depart. A brighter, more respectable future awaits you. You are more fortunate than the others.'

Just then, Elizabeth remembered the Bruce's sisters, kept in cages on castle walls. She remembered Isabella MacDuff, who had bravely scorned her husband and ridden to Scone to crown Robert, by a MacDuff as Scottish tradition demanded. And then there was her stepdaughter, poor innocent Marjorie, who had lost her mother before seeing her father lose all. At ten years of age she had been taken away to a convent, where God alone knew what she had endured.

'I shall do no such thing,' said Elizabeth, suddenly recovering her strength and stepping towards the men as she beheld them defiantly.

They could treat her as they liked, they could subject the Scottish nation to every humiliation. Yet while the Bruce lived she was still his queen, the queen of Scotland.

'Depart forthwith,' she snapped at Bigod, 'and do not speak to me again of receiving any suitors. If it was my father who sent you through his agents in London, tell him not to speak to me again while I remain hostage. For the Bruce is my husband and my king. I took an oath before God which I shall not lightly forego. I am his wife, whatever that makes me in your eyes.'

She turned away from them, while they beheld her for a few moments in stunned silence.

'Ingrate!' yelled Bigod angrily, 'you shall speak to your father soon enough, for our king will soon return the Bruce's head to you on a spike. See what you do then, the young, foolish widow of a mad outlaw and a self-proclaimed king! Do you not see that your husband has no hope of triumph?'

'Truly,' she replied instantly, 'you say that he has none at all?'

'None!', yelled the Constable, 'men say that Edward has four times the Bruce's army!'

'Then tell me, Lords de Dene and Bigod,' cried Elizabeth, as she whirled towards them angrily, 'why has my confinement improved so drastically over the last eight years? In Yorkshire I was served by two crones, furnished with only three clothes and no headgear or linen bed clothing. Yet ever since then my condition has always improved, with ever more servants and even an allowance.'

She beheld the men with blazing eyes.

'Do you think that rumour of my husband's triumphs has not reached me? That I have not heard how he has taken back the whole of his kingdom, save for the castle of Stirling? Are you so confident in his eventual defeat, that you would have his wife ready herself to meet other suitors? Or is this some other cheap trick of the Despensers, to enrich themselves by treating me as chattel? By brokering something that is not even theirs?'

Both Bigod and de Dene tried to hold her stare, yet it was no use.

'You will regret this,' replied the diplomat at last, as he traded stares with the Constable.

Then they were gone, storming out of her room amid grunts and furious muttering, slamming the door behind them as they made their way towards the steps. The hostage produced a deep sigh when they were gone, suddenly overwhelmed by the realisation of her audacity. Her knees shook as she turned towards the window, resting her trembling hands against its sill as she stared outside.

'You should be careful, my lady,' said Matthew behind her, 'yet you did the right thing.'

'Robert,' she sighed, long after her confessor was gone, and the men had ridden back across the bridge, 'will we ever truly be free?'

Chapter VII

ALEXANDER

The New Park and the Carse, 23rd June 1314 AD

Randolph exhaled yet another huge sigh of relief as he marched back with his men towards the New Park. The Scots in his schiltron were all in high spirits as they made back through the trees towards the Borestone where their king awaited him. The summer sun was as bright as it had ever been during the fighting season, which served to further lift the men's mood.

Merely two of their number had perished during their savage fight with Clifford's men, so that the survivors chattered and joked aloud, with each one exaggerating their part in the fight. Most of Randolph's men also wore new armour which had been stripped from the bodies of the dead knights, with many new weapons also forming part of the spoils. Behind them the men led a team of stolen horses.

At the Borestone, the Bruce awaited Randolph with his closest men. They included his brother Eideard, the Black Douglas, Marischal Keith and the Abbott of Inchaffray. Gathered about them were the Scots who formed part of their schiltrons, who all cheered at the appearance of Randolph and his men.

'Upon my oath!' bellowed the Bruce as he strode towards Randolph and wrapped him in a huge embrace, 'you have done yourself much honour, most beloved nephew.'

Marischal Keith also beamed in admiration at Randolph and his squire Gamelin.

'Indeed, you have done yourselves great honour. I have never seen pikemen on the offensive, charging cavalry and breaking through the lines.'

The two men nodded solemnly at the acknowledgement while the Bruce laughed aloud.

'Don't look so modest, you two,' he cried. 'Most beloved nephew, to have broken Clifford's horse with a force of foot. And to have attacked him too! Now men might see that we can stand up to cavalry and also attack horsemen. This calls for a small feast!'

At his back the Scottish king's followers de Kirkpatrick and Cuthbert smiled wryly at this proclamation, seeming more like humans and less like stone statues, while Marischal Keith summoned the Bruce's subalterns to the Borestone. Upon arriving there, the men sat cross-legged alongside each other, pouring heady aqua vitae from a large wooden cask into their helmets. They drank the only way Scots knew how, heavily and jovially.

Meanwhile, Randolph's men dispersed through the rest of the army, bringing heart and courage to every soldier who listened to their accounts of their triumphant attack on mounted knights. Where the men had once feared a valiant if impossible clash with the English, they now dreamt of overcoming the English king's army which had once seemed invincible. Behind them the Bruce's colours of the rampant red lion against a golden banner flapped wildly above the Borestone, seemingly swollen with more pride than ever before.

'twas amazing to behold,' declared Douglas, between large swigs of the brew being shared, 'had we more pikemen, we might even face them.'

'It was indeed great,' replied the Bruce, 'perhaps a sign of days to come. Yet we cannot dream of taking on Edward's numbers in an open field. We bloodied his nose today is all. His archers would scatter the schiltrons like Longshanks did with Wallace at Falkirk. Not to mention the sheer number of men which would surround us on the open plain.'

'Still, it's a shame,' replied Douglas, as he helped himself to another swig, 'so what's the plan?'

'The same as it ever was,' replied the Bruce, 'we burn everything ahead of Edward's army until his supplies run low, while harrying and ambushing his men at every turn.'

'Will it be enough to stop him?' replied Douglas, 'I've never seen so great an army. His leading it around our newly won kingdom shall have Scottish lords leaving our side and openly declaring for him.'

The Bruce shrugged.

'It was ever thus. Yet if we succeed in foiling his army, those same lords will soon declare for us again.'

The Scots were in high spirits well into the evening, while a different mood hung over the army across the meadows which spread before the New Park. The English king had ordered his army to set up camp along the Carse, with many of his men unhappy at having to spend the night upon boggy ground. They were also tired after a hurried march north, scarcely relishing the possibility of having to fight the Scots the following day. It was an even less enticing prospect when word of Sir Henry de Bohun's death quickly spread across the camp, and men learned that Sir Humphrey, Gloucester and Clifford had been repelled by the Bruce's men.

At the edge of the bivouacs, a gaily coloured tent was erected alongside the long train of supply wagons which stretched for twenty miles. By the tent's entrance stood a handful of guards clad in gold and scarlet, while King Edward II sat inside with his head in his hands, gathered with his war council around a wooden trestle table.

The Earl of Gloucester stood opposite them, his generally exuberant and youthful stare dimmed by sheer disappointment. Sir Humphrey and Clifford sat alongside him, their faces ashen after the embarrassment which they had endured when attempting to attack the Scottish pikemen near the New Park. The young king angrily slammed the palm of his hand down on the wooden table. The resulting sound shocked all of the noblemen gathered around him except for the Earl of Pembroke, who sat alongside his king, deeply immersed in thought.

'It's humiliating!' screamed the king, his face turning a scarlet hue.

Clifford did not stir, yet Sir Humphrey and Gloucester shifted in their seats, wary of incurring more of their king's wrath.

'But, Your Majesty -' stammered the Earl of Hereford, perhaps encouraged by the fact that he was the king's brother-in-law.

'You mean to tell me,' shrieked Edward, delighting in having an excuse with which to humiliate an Ordainer who had enabled Gaveston's execution, 'that famous knights like Deincourt or your nephew met their end at the hands of a filthy lowborn Scot?!'

Gloucester could not but nod slowly, with a sinking feeling in the pit of his stomach. Meanwhile Edward shot to his feet and pointed an accusing finger at Sir Humphrey.

'You incompetent cretin,' he screeched, 'I should have you stripped of all titles! So much for your wanting to lead the army!'

The open slur even left Clifford and Pembroke shifting uneasily in their seats, inwardly thanking the Almighty that they were not in the Constable's place. Yet Sir Humphrey surprised them all when he smashed his mailed fist upon the table and shouted back fiercely at his own sovereign and brother-in-law.

'How dare you insult me?!' he barked, having resolved not to accept any more insults, 'when the duel was never my idea?! As for Deincourt, it is him you should be galled at, not me, for underestimating our foes as you do!'

Edward's face turned white as he fell back sheepishly into his seat.

'I am dismayed!' he squealed at last, 'yes, dismayed! Fetch me Owain my Welsh minstrel, with his crwth. That my spirits may somehow be lifted. That I may be ready to lead the attack on the Scots tomorrow morning.'

'But Your Majesty,' said Gloucester, who was renowned for his honesty, 'the men are exhausted after the march north. And in such unforgiving heat too. They need another day to rest before they can be ready to fight.'

Edward snorted aloud as he rose to his feet.

'Are you betraying me, Gilbert de Clare?'

The Earl of Gloucester's face became flustered as he struggled to reply. The insult had been as unfair as it was humiliating.

'Betraying you, Your Majesty? I only stated that the men require a day's rest before they can be expected to fight.'

'Either that,' declared Edward, in a high-pitched screech, 'or you are disloyal! A man who does not respect the wishes of his king!'

'How dare you?' yelled Gloucester after a few moments, as he rose to his feet in outrage with his hand dropping to his sword, 'you only say that because you blame me for Gaveston's death!'

'Perhaps I do!' yelled the king, without batting an eyelid.

Gloucester turned as red as Pembroke had ever seen him, with his hands trembling before he finally managed to speak.

'On the morrow, Your Highness, we shall see who is disloyal.'

With that the young nobleman suddenly stormed out of the tent. Edward laughed mockingly at the sight of the departing Gloucester, then turned towards the Earl of Pembroke.

'It appears, Lord Aymer, that you remain the only member of our council who still has his honour intact. Order heralds to spread through the army, to tell the men that today's setbacks were minor and that victory will be ours tomorrow.'

'Certainly, my lord,' replied Pembroke, who was relieved to see his king making off towards his own quarters.

Clifford and Sir Humphrey also departed not long thereafter, mumbling something about needing to prepare for the battle the following day. Pembroke barely noticed their departure. He instead conversed with the other lesser lords who had gathered in the war council's pavilion, after ordering that they be served with food and drink. One of these lords was a Scot named Alexander Seton. He had been less than impressed by the way the English army was led, while being amazed and inspired by the Bruce's triumphs that day. The wily Earl of Pembroke appeared very interested in Seton's thoughts, as he drank from his mazer and stepped closer to the Scottish knight.

'So I hear tell that you hail from this land,' observed Pembroke, with his cold blue eyes carefully studying the Scottish lord.

'You heard true,' replied Seton, warily staring back at the king's lieutenant.

'So tell me about this Bruce,' replied Pembroke, 'what is it about him that makes men follow him? He is both excommunicated and an outlaw, yet seems to have inspired a great courage and discipline in his men.'

Seton said nothing for a few moments, as he gathered his thoughts.

'I do not know him personally. Yet I have heard tales told by my countrymen. After your night attack at Methven he was left with nothing, forced to flee across the wilds with a few loyal followers and to feed on wild whinberries. They say that when he fled to the isle of

Rachrin, he lay alone in a poor hut, dejected after his disastrous first year as King of Scots. He was thinking of abandoning his kingdom and joining the Crusades, when he caught sight of a spider hanging by a long silvery thread from a wooden beam above his head. The spider tried again and again to swing itself to another beam, failing every time.'

'And what is the relevance of this?' asked Pembroke, wondering what Seton was carrying on about.

'They say the spider tried and failed to reach the other beam six times, which was the same number of times that the Bruce had tried to fight the English and failed. They say the Bruce pledged to try to free Scotland again, if the spider succeeded in its seventh attempt to swing to the next beam. Which it did.'

'Madness!' scoffed Pembroke, 'what utter hogwash. And do you believe that the Bruce would be crazy enough to be inspired by something like that?'

'He was crazy enough to fight de Bohun alone today.'

Pembroke fell silent a few moments, then spoke again.

'Indeed, Lord Seton, perhaps you speak truth. He can be impulsive. I remember him flirting relentlessly with the ladies in Longshanks' court, and he always led the charge in any games or sports held in the palace in London. He even subdued rebellious Scots on behalf of Longshanks, leading a life of great privilege while his own people suffered at home. Then one day, after a violent skirmish with some Scottish rebels, he sat down to eat with blood spattered hands in the presence of other nobles! Do you believe it? They say the Earl of Surrey pointed at him and yelled "look at that Scotsman eating his own blood."'

Seton was shocked by this revelation, wondering how Scots ever fought for people who treated them like that. Then he remembered that he himself formed part of the English army. He also realised that Pembroke was still watching him intently.

'They say he fled the company of English noblemen and rode to a nearby church, where he begged the Lord to forgive him for his sins against his countrymen. It was not long afterwards that he brokered his pact with the Red Comyn, a pact which all but cost him his life in London. Indeed, he was fortunate to get away, for Longshanks wanted him dead. Then he met the Red at Dumfries and slew him in a church.'

Seton nodded vigorously, for he did not wish to hear the story of the Bruce slaying Comyn again. It had been mentioned so many times by the English in recent days, although he had privately also heard tell how the Red had betrayed his secret pact with the Bruce to Longshanks. Yet with the Earl of Pembroke and other English lords still staring at him intently, Seton felt that he should utter some expression of outrage.

'Indeed, he can be impulsive.'

'Very impulsive,' replied Pembroke with a wide grin, then added 'yet is he impulsive enough to face us on the field?'

Seton was taken aback.

'Surely even the Bruce is not that mad?'

'I wonder,' whispered Pembroke, 'yet we should hope that he will attempt insanity tomorrow and take on an army at least three times larger than his own.'

'Should we hope for it?' asked Seton, still impressed by the Scots' triumphs that day.

'Of course we should,' snapped Pembroke, 'otherwise it will be many long days being hampered and attacked by Scots all across the land, while we waste many days attempting to find the Bruce in the wilds. He has perfected the art of raiding and hiding, so that many long and agonising months await us if he does not show tomorrow.'

'Of a certainty,' replied Seton, 'his taking to the field would be our preferred outcome.'

'Perhaps,' replied Pembroke, 'we could at least try to make sure of it?'

Seton looked at the earl, who met his stare and grinned ever more widely.

As darkness set in, the Bruce rose to his feet and told his lieutenants that they would abandon the New Park before dawn to keep a step ahead of the English army. Yet after the stirring events of the day, not all of his subalterns were happy to hear it.

'We should have at them, Robert!' declared his brother angrily, 'each of our men feel ten foot tall after today's triumphs.'

'They are too many, Eideard,' said the Bruce, 'and what of their archers? They will scatter the footmen, which shall leave us defence-less before the cavalry charge. Did you not see how many mounted knights they have?'

Randolph and the Black Douglas said nothing as the brothers argued for almost an hour, with Eideard seeking to convince the Bruce that the invaders were there for the taking. A few of the lords could not help wondering if Eideard's insistence was due to his entering a pact with Stirling's governor many months earlier.

'We risk all by taking to the field,' said the Black Douglas at last, 'one bad defeat will cost us everything, whereas we know the surrounding country. We can retain our strength for as long as we need to.'

'And lose all that we have won to date?' retorted Eideard, 'only Stirling and Bothwell remain beyond our grasp. I say let us take to the field and break our enemies. So they have cavalry, did you not see how Randolph charged them earlier today?'

Randolph said nothing, while secretly hoping that Eideard's insistence be ignored.

The English are simply too many, he thought, *Eideard must accept the threat to the footmen posed by the Welsh archers.*

Just then, great cries were heard at the edge of the wood, where the New Park met with the old Roman road.

'What is it?' asked the Bruce, as a man yelled in the distance.

'A rider approaches! A knight from the English camp!'

'What is this?' asked the Bruce, staring at his brother and other lieutenants in bafflement.

The Lord of the Isles piped up at the Scottish king's shoulder.

'Another knight arrived to challenge you to a duel?'

The Bruce ignored him as he and his lieutenants made their way down towards the edge of the wood. There they made out a mailed rider dismounting from his horse, while Scottish footmen snarled at him and rested the points of their swords against his plate armour.

'Leave him be,' called out the Bruce, with the Scots instantly obeying their king's order.

A clanking sound was issued as the knight fell onto one knee and bowed deeply, then raised his head and lifted his visor. Robert could not make out the man's features in the growing dusk, but the man's voice sounded familiar.

'My king.'

'Seton?' exclaimed the Bruce, 'it cannot be you. What are you doing here?'

The men had known each other in the English king's court when they were younger, also sharing close friends before the Bruce had fled Longshanks' ire many years earlier.

'Indeed, it is I, my king,' replied Seton, 'and I am here to urge you to seize your destiny tomorrow.'

'What do you mean?' asked the Bruce, while his companions regarded the Scottish knight in dumbfounded awe, 'do you not serve the English crown?'

'No longer, Your Highness,' said the knight, rising to his feet, 'for after your exploits upon the field today, I now declare for you. I can see that it is only through your leadership that we will reclaim our land. And I tell you that the English camp is leaderless, with its men possessed of low spirits. They are exhausted after their long march north in baking heat, now forced to sleep upon the marshy, unpleasant ground of the Carse.'

The Bruce pondered over these words for a few moments, then spoke to Seton again.

'Why do you tell me this?'

'I tell you this,' replied Seton, 'because you shall never again be gifted with such a moment. The English wish you to take the field, so arrogant and confident are they of their victory. Pembroke has promised me much fortune and status, were I to ride to you and persuade you to attack the English tomorrow. Yet I swear on my father's grave, my king, that should you take the field, you will surely triumph. Of this I am certain. You may keep me hostage here while you make the attempt tomorrow, have me hung, drawn and quartered if you fail. However I swear upon all that is holy, that tomorrow is the moment you have striven towards for years. A time to finally set Scotland free.'

The Bruce appeared taken aback, then turned to Angus MacDonald.

'Have your men lead this knight away. They should not treat him roughly, yet I must ponder over what he has said to me.'

The Lord of the Isles instantly ordered his Islemen to do their king's bidding. Seton calmly followed his captors without protest, to the place in the woods where he was to be detained.

'So what do you think?' asked the Bruce, turning to his lieutenants.

'It's a ruse,' replied Douglas.

'Yes, it is part of a ruse,' said Randolph, 'otherwise how would the man have reached us? Yet he is also a knight and has declared for you. I am myself concerned about taking the field tomorrow, yet I do not think that he speaks false.'

'I remember mention of Alexander Seton,' said Eideard, 'men say that he is an honourable knight.'

The Bruce nodded to them and stepped towards the Roman road, viewing the land before him which was further obscured by dusk. He was worried that the English knights would outflank his army if he committed to the field of battle. He could imagine the huge tussle as long pikes were driven into the mailed horsemen, while the knights attempted to break through the hedgerows again and again from all sides.

If only there were some way to wedge them between two boundaries. Just like Wallace trapped the English forces on Stirling Bridge.

Then he noticed the glint of the Pelstream to his left, and the Bannock burn to his right. As well as the fires of the English encampment between the two rivers.

If I make the first move, they would be caught between them. But then what of the archers?

As he turned to stare at Seton's nickering horse, the thought struck him that riders always towered above pikemen, just as they had done that morning.

A shield of riders. Maybe...maybe...

The Bruce's men were shocked when he issued a mad laugh in the growing darkness. His brother Eideard was first to recover his composure, then queried the cause of the Scottish king's mirth.

'It just had to be Stirling,' was all the Bruce would say, between nervous chuckles, for a few times thereafter.

Chapter VIII

BANNOCKBURN

Field of battle, 24th June 1314 AD

Edward frowned impatiently as the knave tightened the straps at the back of his greaves. He was a beautiful young man from Kent, with soft hands and slender and nimble fingers, so that Edward barely noticed the deft movements which strapped the armour to his body. Yet the English king had no time or mind for handsome youths that morning, since he was resolved to meet any attack which the Scots might attempt on his force.

For too long have people compared me to father, he thought, *he who gave Piers to me and then took him away. Yet today people will learn that father could never lose with the army at his disposal. And once the Scots are crushed I will return to England and deal with the Ordainers.*

His bunched up fist shook at the thought of the Ordainers. They also reminded him of Gaveston, so that his eyes misted up again and a hot tear slid down his cheek.

You should have been here with me. Yet you will be avenged. After the Bruce, I'll turn on Lancaster, Sir Humphrey and all the rest of them. I'll have them torn apart like the insolent traitors they are.

He stared admiringly at the plate on his arms, which had been polished so well that he could make out his reflection in it. After the knave placed the crown on his head, Edward made his way out of his tent, striding over towards where his horse awaited him. It was a cold air he breathed, with the first greyness of dawn revealing the meadow ahead which ran all the way to the New Park.

Scottish dawns. Horrible things.

He was unused to being roused so early, so he hoped that the Bruce was encouraged enough by the previous days' triumphs to attempt a crazed attack on the English army. Yet as the king was helped onto his horse, he could see no sign of the Scots across the plain.

Perhaps the Bruce is no longer such a fool, after all. Shame.

Behind him he could hear the groans and clank of armour from the Carse, as nobles and commoners alike readied for whatever the day threw at them. As he kicked his steed towards the pavilions, he noticed Pembroke riding towards him, with his squires and pages hurrying after him.

'Hail, Your Majesty.'

The king regaled Pembroke with the slightest nod, since his lieutenant had always been loyal to him, although he had not kept Gaveston safe.

'Are the archers ready?' asked Edward.

'They are,' replied Pembroke, squinting at the king's shining armour, 'five thousand of the kingdom's finest bows, from Wales, the Midlands and the North.'

'Good. Have them take to the field while Gloucester readies the horse. Let's break them up with a few volleys if their pikes try their mad charge again.'

'Indeed, Your Majesty,' replied Pembroke, then started when something caught his eye across the meadow.

From within the trees of the New Park, there slowly advanced three large divisions of men, who took up the whole width of the field between the streams.

'Madness,' gasped Pembroke.

'What? Will yonder Scots fight?' asked the king, as a grin grew upon his face, 'summon the others!'

'Surely sire,' said a passing knight named Sir Ingram de Umfraville, 'but indeed this is the strangest sight I ever saw, for Scotsmen to take on the whole might of England by giving battle on hard ground.'

'Madness,' said Pembroke, glad that he had lured out the Bruce, 'it shall be a slaughter.'

Then he and the king slammed their heels into their mounts' flanks and thundered towards where Lord Talmadge was rallying the English horse. The highest lords of England were already gathered among the many flying pennons and banners which bedecked the English side of the field. They had all waited many weeks for this day, which would live long in the songs. Sir Humphrey was already acting like he would lead the whole cavalry division himself, while Clifford seemed possessed of a furious energy as he threw himself into organizing the cavalry formation while barking his head off at the men.

Pembroke spared a glance for the footmen who were being gathered into various divisions. They all appeared bleary-eyed with long faces, being still worn out from the long march north and a miserable night spent slapping midges on the wretched boggy Carse. The lieutenant was suddenly reminded of Gloucester's warning the previous day, and he returned his attentions to the neighing and loud clops issued by the milling mounts.

Where is Gloucester?

He quickly scanned the various coat of arms and banners, yet he could not make out any sign of the young earl. For a moment he feared that quarrels over who should lead the cavalry would be resumed, so that he hastened back towards the direction of the king, intent on dispelling any argument between Edward and Sir Humphrey. Yet he was already too late, for the two were at it again like cat and dog. Sir Humphrey insisted on leading the cavalry charge, while Edward shrieked that the Constable would keep his place and follow orders when Gloucester appeared.

'I do not know what is keeping him,' fumed the king, jerking his head left and right, 'yet when he appears I want him to lead.'

'This is a disgrace, Your Majesty!' yelled his brother-in-law, who was already turning a darker hue of scarlet.

'We will need more than one leader for the horse,' declared Pembroke.

He reined his steed in between the two quarrellers, when the king seemed taken by something happening across the field.

'They kneel for mercy!' exclaimed Edward, pointing to the Scots across the meadows, who had all fallen onto one knee.

Just then, Sir Ingram spoke up again from among the gathered lords on horseback.

'For mercy yes, but not from you: from God for their sins. These men will win all or die.'

'So be it,' shrugged the king, feeling suddenly confident that he would soon be returning to England, 'sound the trumpets!'

As he knelt to receive a blessing from the Abbot of Inchaffray, the Bruce could make out the formation of the English army as the growing daylight revealed their positions like a raised curtain. The size of the army confirmed what had already been reported by the Bruce's scouts. Before the main host of invaders was a force of two thousand knights who would be led by either Gloucester or Sir Humphrey, although the spies' reports were conflicting. These armoured riders had brought about all of the Scots' previous defeats on the field, since Scotland could never hope to muster enough cavalry to rival the force of English knights.

The mounted warriors stood proud, plumed and shimmering in the growing sunlight, with their colourful surcoats depicting fierce creatures such as dragons and lions. The king of England's army had been financed through a large loan from the Pope, so that knights from France, Brittany, Poitou, Guienne and Germany had also rallied to his banner.

The Bruce was certain that the English knights eyed his footmen with contempt, regardless of his minor triumphs the previous day.

They will be certain that once we take the field, they shall trample us like so many times before.

Behind the mounted knights stood thousands of foot soldiers, said to be around twenty-five thousand strong. Many of them consisted of battle-scarred professional troops who were divided into ordered ranks of pikemen, swordsmen and axemen. They also included hundreds of Ulstermen from Ireland who had been raised and transported by the Bruce's own father-in-law, the Earl of Ulster.

There was also a large division of infantry led by King Edward II himself. This formed the majority of footmen and consisted mostly of thousands of unprofessional reserves, tenants and youths who had little interest in the upcoming fight. Yet although the Bruce knew that they were exhausted and had spent a wretched night attempting to sleep in the Carse, they were many in number and made the English army look both huge and intimidating.

Edward's host was a fearsome sight, so that the elderly Abbot of Inchaffray strode among the kneeling Scots along with other priests, reciting the lesson of the day to give them strength in their cause,

Comfort ye, comfort ye
Speak ye comfortably to Jerusalem
And cry unto her that her warfare is accomplished

All throughout, the Bruce's eye was fixed on the Welsh archers across the field. He could make them out to his left, barely six yards away from the main body of English knights. There were thousands of them, all expertly trained. Soon they would be poised and ready to shoot clothyard arrows among the Scottish pikemen, to break their formations before the knights reached them. Their shafts had caused havoc among the Scots at Falkirk, sixteen years earlier, when the seemingly invincible William Wallace had been defeated. The English knew the tactic always worked, and they had already blamed the previous day's setbacks on the absence of archers.

All of the Bruce's men were fired up by the previous day's triumphs, as well as their months of training received from their king in the Torwood. Each of the men were handpicked Highlanders or renowned Scottish warriors, each ready to die for the cause. Even Alexander Seton, an able-bodied knight of some renown, had been ordered to join the reserves behind the Gillies Hill, so as not to disrupt the carefully prepared maneuvers which the Scots had practiced for months.

As his men muttered words of encouragement to each other, the Bruce rode haughtily before them and raised his hand for silence. Upon his leather jerkin he wore a shirt of chain mail, and by his side de Kirkpatrick and Cuthbert brandished their jagged maces, with Angus Macdonald scowling openly behind them. In the king's own hand, his men could make out the huge double-handed broadsword which had once belonged to William Wallace. It was a revered weapon which the great patriot and martyr had wielded during his first fight against the English at Lanark. Its blade glinted as it caught the early light of the sun, a massive length of steel almost five feet long. It would take an expert warrior to wield it effectively, a strong man with the perfect balance and timing to swing it through anything and anyone.

At the sight of the blade, the Scots were overcome with patriotic fervor as many of them recalled Wallace's incredible triumph against the English at Stirling Bridge, while also recalling his cruel execution at Longshanks' order. The Bruce regarded his haggard men who looked to him with stained and solemn faces, and the silence which spread among them was almost holy.

'Sirs,' he declared, 'our enemies are moved only by desire for dominion. But we fight for our lives, our children, our wives and the freedom of our country. On this day, I ask and pray that with all your strength, without cowardice or alarm, you meet the foes so boldly that those behind them shall tremble. You could have lived quietly as slaves, but because you longed to be free you are with me here. And to gain that end you must be valiant, strong and undismayed.'

The Bruce's voice never wavered as he beheld his men who were rapt as they stared back at him. Then the Scottish king broke into a rare smile.

'I know not what more to say. You know what honour is. For those who fight manfully, I promise by virtue of my royal power that I will pardon all crimes against the Crown. I shall also forgive all taxes due by their heirs!'

The Scots could hardly believe what they were hearing, so that for a moment most thought he had gone mad. Then their king was almost thrown off his horse when his men raised their arms and issued a united roar of defiance which struck a deep unease in the hearts of their distant enemies. Suddenly even the English king was not as sure of victory as he had once been. Alongside him Pembroke shifted warily in his saddle, while the other Earls glimpsed at each other in fear.

The Bruce proceeded to deploy his troops as he had planned the previous night. He ordered his small company of archers from the Ettrick Forest to take to the field, then ensured that the schiltrons in the van consisted of Thomas Randolph's five hundred pikemen. Eideard, the king's brother, commanded the right division of a thousand strong. Alongside him stood the huge Lindsay, a former companion of Wallace, who had been ordered by the king to protect his brother. To the left of Randolph's division, the young Walter Steward nominally led his own squares of a thousand foot, which were in truth led by the Black Douglas.

Alongside this assortment of troops was a squadron of five hundred horsemen under the command of Marischal Keith. Behind them all, the king of Scotland took charge of his own division of two thousand men, with his movements always shadowed by de Kirkpatrick and Cuthbert. His schiltrons were made up of men from twenty clans of Highlanders, MacDonald Islemen, as well as the Bruce's own men from Carrick, Kyle and Cunningham. In all, the Scottish army numbered six thousand men, almost a third of the English invaders.

At the Bruce's command, Randolph's schiltrons made their way towards the enemy, with men marching in step with all the slow sturdiness of a battering ram. Eideard and Black Douglas' phalanxes flanked those of the king's nephew, as they marched along at the same slow yet determined pace, with all footmen holding their pikes at the ready. Meanwhile the Bruce held back, as he slowly shadowed the steps of his three commanders with the large force at his back.

The armies were within a few hundred yards of each other, with the Scots' force flanked by a ravine and a river. As the English trumpets were sounded, the English king and Pembroke suddenly realised that they had not yet agreed who would lead the cavalry charge instead of Gloucester.

'At your command!' yelled Sir Humphrey from among the mounted knights, again and again. However Edward ignored him while Pembroke prayed that the king would finally see reason and allow his brother-in-law to lead the horse. Then their jaws dropped when Gloucester suddenly rode out before them atop a black stallion. The young Earl did not wear any surcoat or colours of his house.

'Where were you?' shrieked the king, visibly enraged by the young Earl's delayed appearance.

Gloucester flashed him a look of unmasked hatred.

'You called me disloyal before these here knights,' he declared, 'yet I will meet your accusation with deeds and not words! I shall not hide behind the colours of my house or my rank, for by arms alone will I recover my honour!'

So saying, he whirled his mount about and thundered off towards the Scots. He never once hailed to the other riders, yet Clifford was already charging after him, the seasoned veteran having long chomped at the bit to take to the fight. To his horror, Edward could see the son of the Red also charging after them, before hundreds of knights next thundered away from the Carse of Balquhiderock.

'They're...they're gone...' muttered the king to his lieutenant.

'Utter madness,' sighed Pembroke, as he watched the disorderly advance of the knights.

They seemed to be competing in a horse race, attempting to outrun each other as they thundered on towards the New Park.

'To me!' yelled Sir Humphrey, both flustered and angered that he had not been first across the field.

Mounted knights stared askance at the Constable as he galloped towards the Black Douglas' division, then one by one they each dug in their spurs and also made off.

As the knights closed the distance between them and the Scots, the Welsh archers readied their bows, with their arrows already fitted.

'At my order!' yelled their commander, a seasoned veteran named Madoc, who sprang sideways as a bolt hit the ground before his feet.

'Argh!' cried another Welshman behind him, as an arrow ripped through his throat and sent him tumbling across the grass.

'What madness is this?' cried Madoc, as he lay on the ground with arrows striking the earth about him, 'archers taking aim at archers? How dare they?'

Across the field, he could make out the Bruce's company of archers fitting arrows to their bows and taking aim at the Welsh again.

'By Christ's blood,' snarled the enraged Madoc, as his friends and other bowmen died around him.

He snatched up his bow and returned to his feet, barking another command.

'Let them have a volley!'

A surge of hate flooded Gloucester as he rammed his spurs into his mount again and again, then stood in his stirrups and beheld the Scots marching towards him.

Anytime now, the arrows will scatter them. I'll cut them all down.

The wind whistled through his hair, for he had no need for a helmet. The outcome was so inevitable that he could not wait to start bringing his blade down upon the sheep-fiddling, uncouth and ragged vermin. He, Gilbert de Clare, would teach them single-handedly what it meant to take up arms against the king of England. With gritted teeth he recalled the Scots' cheers the previous day, when he was forced to retreat with his riders along the Roman road.

Yet today there will be no quarter given. Scottish filth, the moment they break I shall be their worst nightmare. Send them all scurrying into the hills.

He could not hear the pounding of hoofs behind him, so determined was he to bathe himself in Scottish blood before presenting the head of the Bruce to his king.

I'll show him who's disloyal, throw the Bruce's head right at his feet.

The men before him were closer now, so that he could already make out the whites of their eyes.

None of them are laughing now, just look at the poor fools making a stand.

He dug his spurs into his mount's flanks again, as the creature issued another loud whinny and managed a faster gallop, tearing up the grass underfoot as it thundered towards the slowly rising hedge-row of spears.

To Eideard, it felt like the very earth beneath his feet was shaking, with a growing wall of every colour imaginable quivering before him, melded with a glare of shining steel. So that the solitary horseman careering towards his men was almost a relief on the eyes, for the rider wore neither colours nor crest.

Perhaps he's drunk?

As the rider drew nearer, the Earl of Carrick realised that Clifford followed at a great distance behind the charging rider, with other knights who included the Red's son. The Bruce's brother traded a quick glance with Lindsay, who was as baffled as he was.

Who is that?

Then Eideard could make out the whites of the rider's eyes, the contorted features and the gritted teeth. The rider seemed at once almost familiar, with only a few yards remaining between him and the schiltron. Eideard's pikemen knew what to do without receiving any command. For they had trained for months in the Torwood, with the Bruce putting them through gruelling paces day after day and demanding the utmost discipline. Yet the Bruce's brother had never imagined that their first encounter would be with one solitary rider.

Is this some kind of trick?

Eideard was half tempted to urge his men to spare the man's life, until he saw the rider's lance being lowered. Then he barked at his men to be wary, yet the pikes were already held forward, creating a row of stakes fitted with the sharpest steel in the world. The rider's eyes seemed to suddenly widen, having finally realised that he was galloping hard towards certain death. For a moment Gloucester almost tugged at his reins, then refrained from showing cowardice. He could not prove

Edward right. The king had called him a traitor before the entire war council, he would at least be remembered for a mad act of bravery.

The arrows, he thought desperately, *where are the God-forsaken arrows?*

Amid the hideous splintering of wood, the earl was instantly flung headfirst into the pikes. Eideard grimaced as a front pikeman expertly lanced the rider's throat, skewering him like a salmon in mid-flight as he flew off his horse, then hoisted the rider and dropped him onto a half dozen glinting pikeheads. The knight was left hanging in the air like a piece of skewered mutton, Eideard thought drily. Then the razor-sharp blades sliced through the rider's body, so that his blood soaked head suddenly dangled right in front of the Bruce's brother.

'Good Lord,' said the younger Bruce.

'What happened?' asked Lindsay.

'We've killed bloody Gilbert de Clare, the Earl of Gloucester,' remarked Eideard, then remembered how Gloucester's stepfather, Ralph de Monthermer, had rescued his brother from Longshanks years earlier, when he had sent Robert twelve pence and a pair of spurs.

'Why wasn't he wearing his colours?' asked Lindsay, then added 'waste of a good ransom.'

Yet Eideard's attention had already turned back onto the battlefield, where he could make out Clifford bearing down on them. A steady stream of knights charged after the Lord Warden, which was fast turning into a flood. The almighty thunderstorm of beating hooves meant that the Scots could barely hear each other's yells as the riders grew nearer. Eideard roared at his men to stand their ground and to ready their pikes again.

'Hold!' he cried, making out the slits in Clifford's visor, with the stench of piss already thick in the air as some younger men struggled to master their fear.

As the knights grew in size, he knew that the impending impact would decide almost everything. No matter how much the Scottish king had trained his men, only nerve would determine if the schiltrons held. It was why the men were hand-picked, fighters who had crossed castle moats with the Bruce at the dead of night, with ice cold water up to their necks. Men who had scaled the walls of Edinburgh with Randolph at the dead of night, or who had hidden with Douglas on Palm Sunday before famously reducing the Douglas Castle into the horrific 'Douglas Larder.'

'Men who would die for you, Robert,' whispered Eideard beneath his breath, as Highlanders before him struck the ground with their pike butts and planted their feet on the ends of them.

Then the Bruce's younger brother closed his eyes, as the approaching Clifford lowered his lance and stood in his stirrups.

If God had torn the world asunder, Randolph doubted that the sound would have been as great as that of the knights crashing into Eideard's schiltrons.

'Holy Virgin,' gasped Gamelin at his shoulder.

All of Randolph's division looked right to see knights hanging from pike ends, amid loud screams of impaled men and horses who lay thrashing in the grass. Then their attentions were returned to the infinite wall of steel and lances which advanced upon them and Douglas' division to their left.

Randolph drew a deep breath as the figures grew larger, while the Scottish archers turned tail and fled behind Douglas' lines, keen to escape the cavalry charge while more Welsh arrows thudded into the grass behind them. Randolph drew his sword and readied to order a halt, with his men still marching forward in orderly formation with all the pluck of roosters and the sturdiness of an ox cart.

'Been good, Tam!' shouted Gamelin, so that Randolph almost turned to acknowledge him.

Then nothing else could be heard, not even the beating of his heart, as his ears were filled with the growing beat of hooves. It was like a field of raging drums, as blue, yellow and scarlet surcoats closed in. On an impulse, he stole a quick glance right, where he saw Clifford hanging dead from the pikes of Eideard's men, then looked left where he could make out Sir Humphrey's colours. The Constable of England led hundreds upon hundreds of knights towards Douglas' men.

'God help us,' he sighed, though he never heard his own words, nor the sword ringing from his scabbard.

Pembroke stared on in wonder as the men of the Bruce seemed to disappear behind the infinite number of knights on horseback. The crash and splintering of Scottish spears sounded like distant cracks of lightning, which somehow cut through the almighty beat of horses' hooves. The standards borne by the Scottish squares appeared to wobble, then vanish behind the figures of men and horses which filled the air above the Scottish footmen. Yet there were still hundreds of mailed riders who had not yet reached the enemy, as yard upon yard of stallions' and geldings' hindquarters drew closer together and crashed into the riders ahead of them.

'Cut them down like grass!' cried Edward gleefully and shaking his fist before him, 'we'll be on our way home tonight, Lord Aymer!'

Pembroke was unsure what to say, as he held his gloved hand above his eyes to shield them from the sun's glare. The knights' mounts did not seem to have become any smaller, with the hoof beats slowly dying out as the sound of screams and desperate cries filled the air. Hundreds of riders could next be seen running sideways into the two rivers, or careering towards gaps among the horses. All the while an infernal din of battle rose as if from the depths of hell, as shrieking, riderless horses galloped back towards the English camp.

'Is it over?' asked the king, looking to his lords, 'it is over isn't it? Isn't it?'

Yet none would answer. It was hard to tell what was happening apart from riders veering away from the pikemen and charging them again, only to disappear into a mass of squirming bodies upon the ground.

'Why were the Scots still holding?' asked Pembroke, then looked right and made out the Welsh archers shooting bolts at the Scottish archers behind Douglas' division.

'What are those fools doing?' he snapped, instantly galloping off towards the bowmen.

As he got closer to the Welshmen, he raised his shield against the shower of Scottish arrows. One of them tore through the targe yet did not reach him, as the sickening thud of arrowheads struck the ground about him. Pembroke lowered his shield and kicked his horse towards a Welsh captain who howled at his fellows to take aim again.

'What are you fools doing?!' cried the earl, hardly believing what he was seeing.

'We are giving the Scots' archers a volley,' replied the surprised Madoc, 'they've been taking aim at us since the battle began!'

Pembroke was entirely taken aback by the revelation.

Damn Bruce. Now that caught me off guard.

'Your orders were to take aim at the schiltrons!' he roared, fearing another volley from the Scots at any minute.

Madoc waved at his men to loosen their arrows, then turned back to the earl.

'So we aimed at the Scots' archers instead. What of it?!'

'Follow your orders!' shrieked the earl, as spittle ran down his chin, 'take aim at the bloody schiltrons instead!'

Madoc turned back towards the sight of the horsemen desperately attempting to break through the pikemen. Upon realising his folly, he swiftly urged his men to take aim at the Scottish pikemen instead. Pembroke quietly noted that he had a better view of proceedings alongside the archers, as he saw the Scots closing in whenever a charging knight managed to momentarily break through their formation. The echelon structure of the Bruce's pikemen was seemingly impregnable, although the battle was not yet lost. Pembroke hoped that the sheer number of mounted knights would eventually wear down the phalanxes, so that the Bruce's men would be spent enough before the English footmen finally joined the struggle.

'Now!' cried Madoc, as the Welshmen released their shafts.

The sky overhead was soon filled with hundreds of clothyard arrows, that flew over the heads of the English knights. Yet to his growing dismay, Pembroke saw that the mounted warriors formed a steel shield as they towered over the pikemen, so that not a single arrow found its target. Many of the Welsh were cut down by Scottish arrows as they again attempted to strike the pikemen, yet it was all in vain.

'It is no use!' cried Madoc, as he gestured towards the next volley that went over the combatants.

Pembroke sighed aloud and turned towards the Pelstream which kept the English army from spreading right.

'I'll be back,' he gasped, then galloped towards the river to seek out a crossing.

Lindsay could not believe it. The Bruce's brother was actually grinning widely as more of the English knights landed upon the pikes. A few hundred knights wheeled away from the square to attempt yet another charge.

'Close ranks!' cried the Bruce's brother, then roared, 'at them!'

His men grunted and groaned as they lowered their pikes and shoved their way forward, trampling over the torn bodies of kicking horses and dead knights. Eideard marvelled at his men's resolve, for they had withstood an inhuman battering of charging mounts for well over two hours, yet still had stomach for the fight. Slowly but surely they patiently closed ranks and held together tightly, barely missing a step as they shoved the riders ahead of them backwards, foot by precious foot, until they reached the Bannockburn. Then another loud whinny was heard, as hundreds of horsemen wheeled about and readied to charge Eideard's squares again.

At the centre of the great conflagration, Randolph wiped the blood from his face and ran his sword through the neck of another unhorsed knight. His sword arm was burning and he could barely feel it, nor could he feel his legs for the number of times he had raced through the ranks with other soldiers to slay unhorsed riders. The sheer amount of killing had taken a massive toll on them, with Randolph's throat red raw from heavy breathing while sweat dripped freely out of his sleeves. The stench about him was terrible, he was uncertain whether it was just blood or dung or piss.

Probably all three mingled with horse sweat and the stench of bodies.

Then he dispelled the thought from his mind, running back to the middle of the schiltron as yet another wave of horsemen crashed into the struggling pikemen. Then it was back at the gaily coloured bodies again, finding chinks and gaps in armour through which he could slip his sword point. He had disposed of four more, then stopped to feel sick and slew another two, when he felt someone tugging at his sleeve. He turned to face his squire, who was also blood-spattered and slack jawed from sheer exhaustion, his helmet long lost and his hair scattered all over the place.

'Wha--?' hissed Randolph, for it was all he could manage.

'Less this time,' rasped Gamelin.

Randolph shrugged for it meant nothing to him. There had to be someone he had not yet killed. Then there came the annoying tugging on the sleeve again.

'Whaaa-?' he hissed, in dire need of a drink of water.

Gamelin gestured right, where Randolph saw his uncle Eideard's schiltrons ramming their mounted assailants and pushing them back towards the Bannockburn. Suddenly their cause made sense to him again.

'Close ranks!' he cried, 'at them! At them!'

Standing within the schiltron closest the Pelstream, Douglas wished he could somehow reach the Earl of Hereford. Yet Sir Humphrey remained just out of reach, even when Douglas had barked at his men to push forward, to join the advance of those divisions commanded by Randolph and Eideard. Amid great roars of elation, the pikemen took advantage of the knights' hesitation and the lessening of their numbers, as they moved forward without ever losing their shape.

Two months of training, thought Douglas, *and Robert got them moving like the Flemish at Courtrai.*

His awe was cut short when an arrow slammed into the ground before him, causing him to lose balance and fall onto the pikeman ahead of him. A jabbing elbow caught him in the nose, so that his hand was spattered with blood after he reached for his face. Loud cries of agony were heard around him as Scottish pikemen fell to their knees, with arrow shafts sticking out of them. The men had been straining at the push of pike for hours, battered by countless charges of knights, so that it was all they could do to keep on their feet.

This volley is the last thing we need.

Douglas returned to his feet, pushing through the clash of steel upon steel, the snapping of spearshafts, the groans of the wounded and the screams of disemboweled horses. He then reached the edge of his leftmost schiltron, where he saw to his horror that the Welsh archers had forded the Pelstream and were taking aim from beyond the stream. He hurried back to where Walter Stewart was busy stabbing an unhorsed rider, and pulled the young knight from the shoulder.

'Where is Robert?' he gasped, pointing back at the Pelstream so that Walter also saw the archers, 'where is he?'

Then a great bugle blast was heard, followed by loud cries as the Bruce finally played his full hand and led his two thousand pikemen towards the engaged divisions before him. He also released a runner who bore urgent orders to the cavalry division of Marischal Keith, who awaited the king's orders with his five hundred knights at the edge of the New Park. As his men marched steadily towards the divisions ahead of them, the king felt a curious relief. For hours he had watched his men execute his orders to perfection, while he itched to join in the fray.

'Pick your timings, my boy,' his beloved grandfather, Robert the Competitor, had always told him as they sat across each other at the chess table.

Robert had ignored him, since he had been hasty as a boy, too quick to commit his knights to win petty pawns.

'Time will teach you, if no one else will,' said his grandfather with a sigh, as he quickly snatched up the horse pieces, 'you are too rash, Robert my lad.'

Yet on this crucial day, the Bruce had picked his timing to perfection, with his combined force of Islemen and Highlanders filling the gaps in Douglas' dwindling divisions, while pushing against their exhausted comrades to help them withstand yet another cavalry charge. As another shower of arrows landed amongst his men, he turned his head towards the Pelstream, where he could see the knights of Marischal Keith charging the Welsh archers who broke and fled. Madoc desperately tried to cross the stream while many of his men were cut down.

As he stood back alongside his king, the Earl of Pembroke bit his lip in anger as he watched the slaughter of the bowmen, their numbers virtually useless once hand to hand fighting ensued. As the archers tried to flee, the Scots' horse encircled them, led by their Marischal who stood in his stirrups and swung large, fatal arcs with his sword. It was a rout, with Pembroke left to curse himself for having let the thousand archers position themselves so far from his main force. Everything was happening too quickly, and his only consolation was that his king had not yet realised that his large archery division was being destroyed.

The Bruce grimaced with satisfaction, as he drew his double-hander and readied to draw enemy blood.

'Close in!' he yelled, 'they fail!'

Randolph heard the cry just as the last knights before him were slaughtered, then barked at his pikemen who surged forward, clambering over dead knights and horses towards the trembling English footmen. The Bruce's Islemen and Highlanders pressed in closely after him, roaring their thunderous battle-cries.

Eideard's and the Black Douglas' divisions also charged forward, drawing inhuman strength in their crushing defeat of the English knights. The clash of steel upon steel was enormous as the Scottish flung down their pikes and assaulted the first of the English infantry, who were left stunned by the ferocity of the attack. The Highlanders and Islemen seemed ready to march through hell itself as they tore into the invaders, being soon locked in a vicious struggle with the seasoned English veterans.

Soldiers twice his age appeared before Randolph. The first he cut down with an upward stroke, then chopped the second's face open with a vicious backhander. The third was killed before he had even sighted the king's nephew. With each swing of Randolph's blade an English swordsman died. Behind him Angus *Óg* MacDonald parried the spear thrust of an enormous footman before swinging his axe round into his enemy's head. To their left, Eideard smashed his mace into a soldier's neck and felled another one with a rain of aggressive blows. Just when an Englishman was about to hack him down from behind, Lindsay, who was ever looking out for the Bruce's brother, kicked the Englishman so hard between the legs that he never rose again.

On the far right of the enemy army, nothing stood in the path of Douglas and Walter Stewart, as their body of troops tore through the English and scythed them down like stalks of wheat. The English foot men were overwhelmed. Those of them who had fought in Longshanks' terrible wars in France had never witnessed such a savage onslaught. Within the Carse, the Bruce just about made out the English standard fluttering in the wind.

He knew that the king would be below it, with a crowd of mailed nobles and bodyguards around him. Every now and again the English king himself could be seen setting off at a gallop to rally the English troops whenever they faltered. Edward had often been mocked for his friendship with Gaveston, yet the Bruce noted how the English king fought bravely, with the blows of his mace felling Scots who tried to seize his horse's bridle. Ahead of him the English footmen appeared to be wavering, yet the Scottish king still had a card up his sleeve which he thought would turn the tide.

So he was not surprised when the English troops suddenly stared up at the Gillies Hill in horror. Pembroke saw their faces and also looked towards the distant summit. The earl was overwhelmed by a chilling dismay, when he caught the sight of what appeared to be fresh Scottish army making its way downhill. Ahead of him an English lord spurred his mount and charged off, shrieking 'retreat! Retreat! The battle is lost! The battle is lost!'

They were his last words as a ragged highlander pulled him off his saddle and beat his brains out with a hammer. Yet they were not without effect. Panic spread among the English footmen as all those who heard the cry turned and fled. The Scots pursued them and battered them down, all the while roaring in triumph. Thousands of the beaten soldiers retreated towards King Edward II who beheld them in shock and disbelief.

Upon the Gillies Hill, cries of joy could be heard from the fifteen thousand camp followers who had been mistaken by the English for a fresh army of Scots. Led by the benevolent Abbot of Inchaffray, they made their way down towards the battlefield, with their blankets mounted on tent poles as they observed the havoc which their appearance had caused their enemies.

With a curse, Pembroke seized Edward's bridle and swiftly led him away, with the five hundred knights in the king's bodyguard swiftly encircling them.

'No!' shrieked Edward, suddenly realising his great humiliation and swinging his mace at thin air, 'I cannot leave! We must win!'

Pembroke ignored him as the king's bodyguards closed tightly around the protesting king to ensure he be safely ushered away from the field. Time was of the essence, since the Scots had already reached them, while thousands of leaderless English soldiers ran towards the streams. Edward's bodyguards hastened to cut a path through them, as the king watched his desperate footsoldiers splashing around helplessly and drowning by the hundredfold.

His nostrils filled with the stench of blood, Randolph tirelessly spurred on his men, who worked their way slowly but surely towards the English standard. A head or a limb flew before each stroke of his sword. The English were many in number, yet all of them quailed before him. Meanwhile the Bruce was himself soon in the thick of battle, hacking at the English veterans while his fresh troops swelled the ranks of their fellow countrymen engaged in fevered hand to hand combat. The Bruce charged through a rare gap among Randolph's men, his longsword descending like lightning bolts upon the helmets of the invaders who fell before him like stalks of wheat before a harvester.

'To me! To me! For Scotland! For Scotland!'

His roar whipped up the enthusiasm of every Scot within earshot, and his fury spread through his army like wildfire. The Scots pushed forward undeterred, their arms rising and falling as the mounds of enemy dead rose about them. Ahead of the Bruce, the Highlanders and Islemen glared at their foes through the twirling, flashing melee of sword and axe and spear. They snarled like animals amid the sobbing breathlessness of their victims. The clang and grate of metal and the sharp scream of human agony rose once more as the Scots ran riot on the insane, glorious midsummer day. Amid the infinite scenes of utter madness, the last words of the late William Wallace beat against the Bruce's brain, just before the Scottish patriot's execution in London:

"I could never be a traitor to Edward. For I was never his subject."

Chapter IX

REUNION

Rochester Castle to Scottish borderlands,
24ᵗʰ June 1314 AD

It all seemed quite mad.

At Rochester, they treated her with a grudging respect, verging on reverence. Only two servants were needed to pack her few belongings, so that she was soon dressed in travelling clothes and ready to leave the castle. It was a sunny June day - in fact she did not think that the weather could possibly have been fairer. For the first time in years, the clank of armoured men was not produced by her jailers but by her guards. Yet she had been hostage for so long, that she still refrained from smiling or displaying any outward expressions of joy.

Elizabeth had heard of the rout which had followed Bannockburn, she had no doubt that many of the people who watched her leave had each lost a brother, son or husband, or at least a distant relative at the slaughter which had followed. The Scots had been triumphant, it was a whisper which men shared in incredulous snatches. Many English noblemen had been taken prisoner, so her life was more valuable to her husband's enemies than it had ever been before.

She did not wish to cause offence or risk wrath, for the tidings after Bannockburn hardly seemed possible to her. So she kept her silence as she approached the castle doorway to the courtyard. Her custodian Stephen de Dene stood alongside it, with other petty nobles in his service. As they engaged in a deep bow, she returned the slightest of nods, which was the least acknowledgement she might get away with to avoid being openly rude.

De Dene noticed this but said nothing, although his eyes narrowed in hatred as she walked past him. In the courtyard she could not avoid a quiver of excitement as a horse was brought out to her, with a small smile finally appearing on her face as she mounted it. She was to be accompanied to Yorkshire by a band of a dozen armed riders, with two servants to attend to her daily needs and a purse full of shillings to pay for lodgings, when available, throughout her journey north.

Her heart quickened when her travelling party rode off at a canter, towards the gate of the bawn. As they drew closer, she made out a hooded figure in a cowl, slowly raising a hand in farewell towards her. Almost by instinct, she swiftly drew rein and turned her horse towards the bystander, reining in her steed alongside him. Chafed, rough hands pulled back the hood, revealing the sorrowful face of Brother Matthew. His azure eyes glistened as he fought back his overwhelming sadness and forced a smile on his face.

'Godspeed, my lady,' he managed, his voice husky from recent weeping, 'I wish you all happiness, now you are free.'

Elizabeth looked back at him for a few moments, with their silence and proximity meaning much more than any words could express. They would never forget the time they had spent together, yet they knew they would never see each other again. The queen of Scotland sighed aloud and smiled back at him.

'Thank you,' she said, while hoping that his brothers had not perished at the hands of her husband's men.

He fought back a frown while his lips were pursed tightly together, then smiled one last time before pulling his hood over his head again and stepping back a few paces. Lady de Burgh was already riding back towards her armed escort, who spurred their steeds on again towards the gate at the bawn. It would be a week of riding along Roman roads and unpaved trackways, with rivers forded wherever the old Roman bridges and river crossings had fallen into disrepair. She was glad that they would avoid the palace in London, where rumour told that the English king had not been seen for days on end.

One night they even set up camp under the stars, yet it was early summer and the cold was not overly cruel. Although she missed her conversation with Matthew, Elizabeth stared at the stars above and made out the warlike constellation of Orion the Hunter. She remembered how Robert had first pointed it out to her, so that she could almost imagine him looming over her in the sky. As she closed her eyes to sleep, she was overcome by some unease as she wondered whether the years had changed him. He had always been formidable and single-minded, yet had his constant battling also rendered him cruel?

After many days on the road, they spent the night at the Norman castle at Conisbrough, then proceeded on their way to York. Elizabeth's heart leapt when she saw the distant walls of the city. As they crossed the southern river and rode past the timber-framed shops, she could tell that the whole town was astir.

'It is due to your husband's victory, my lady,' said Alan Glanville, the leader of her armed escort, 'people here still remember the raids of Wallace, almost seventeen years ago.'

Upon entering York Castle, Elizabeth was overjoyed to meet the Bruce's sisters Mary and Christina, as well as her stepdaughter Marjorie who cast a silent, bewildered figure after her years spent at the nunnery.

'You are so grown up, my child,' said Elizabeth, embracing her sullen stepdaughter who barely managed a smile.

The child had endured much on behalf of her father, yet the lady de Burgh hoped that she could look forward to years of relative peace ahead. Although time had taught her that one could never be assured of peace in Scotland.

'And Isabella?' she asked the Bruce's sisters, remembering the brave Lady MacDuff and Countess of Buchan, who had abandoned her husband to crown the Bruce at Scone, to honour the age-old tradition of a MacDuff crowning the Scottish king.

Mary and Christina looked away at the question, so that Elizabeth was suddenly overwhelmed by sadness, having hoped that they would all return to Scotland together. Yet unlike her, Isabella had at Longshanks' order been imprisoned in an outdoor cage for four years, before being moved to the Carmelite friary at Berwick. Elizabeth could not imagine the suffering that the poor woman had endured before returning to live indoors.

In the following days there were many comings and goings to the castle, with the women preferring to reside within the safety of the walls rather than incur the ire of the crowds outside. Then one day the ladies observed the returning Sir Humphrey and other highborn English lords arriving at the castle.

'He looks mad with rage,' noted Christina, yet none of the others spoke.

They were not summoned to meet with any of the returning lords recently released by the Bruce, yet were instead ordered to depart for Scotland forthwith. They left the castle with a larger force of men, led towards their country before being assigned to a division of Scottish soldiers at the border. Thereafter they reached a clearing in a forest, where they dismounted and made out four figures approaching them. In the midday sun, Elizabeth could make out Randolph, young and erudite, yet ever wary. There was Black Douglas, of a wild and feral cast, who eyed them like a wolf. There then followed Eideard Bruce, Earl of Carrick, with a torn face and the picture of defiance. And finally there appeared Robert, larger than life, tallest of all, who beheld them with world-weary brown eyes and a wan smile. His sisters were first to cry aloud in delight, as they ran towards him with his daughter.

He made to speak but could not, as he fell to one knee and wrapped the three of them in an almighty embrace which lasted for long moments. Elizabeth wished it had been her he embraced first, yet deep down she felt a huge relief that he had been reunited with his sisters and daughter. Then Mary and Christina proceeded to embrace their other brother Eideard, while the Bruce fixed his eyes on her like he had done all those years ago in London, when still a popular member of Longshanks' court.

'My king,' she stuttered, tears gathering on her eyelids.

He stood before her, beaming with a roguish charm. His arm was wrapped around the shoulders of his smiling daughter, with his sisters behind them.

'Your husband,' he said.

Then she wept openly as he strode towards her and held her in a tight embrace.

'It is over,' he whispered.

'So many lost,' she managed, trying to keep herself from wailing as tears ran freely.

'It is over,' he repeated.

It was a long embrace but she felt unworthy. She could not imagine how much he had endured, the unspeakable sacrifices to bring them together at this point in time. As if sensing her distress, he slowly held her chin and raised her face towards his. They were the same eyes from all too many years ago, eyes she was once sure she would never behold again. Defiant, untamed and commanding.

'Can it be true?' she said.

His lips were suddenly pressed hard against hers by way of reply, then her head was clutched to his chest as they were united in another embrace. He held her like he would never let her go again.

'We are most fortunate,' she said at last, 'to be free to have this, I mean. Indeed, we are most fortunate.'

She looked up at him and noticed how his eyes blazed madly at her with unrestrained defiance.

'No,' he replied firmly, 'we are most Scottish.'

Historical Note

During my last reading of the manuscript of this novel, the world has been shocked by the invasion of Ukraine by Vladimir Putin. I can hardly believe the timing of this attack, and the similarities between this present-day conflict and the struggle of the Bruce against Scotland's oppressors King Edward I (Longshanks) and his son Edward II. For almost three decades now, we've been bombarded with various icons and idols ranging from Paris Hilton to Jay-Z et al, so that having a latter-day Bruce of sorts (at least as perceived by the Western world) like Volodymyr Zelenskyy dominating the media seems almost like a daydream.

History might not repeat itself, but it certainly does rhyme. I've no doubt that the Bruce, were he still around, would be awed by how surging nationalism, a bitter fight to the last and scenes of so many displaced, suffering people have torn through all the mindless pop culture on our tv (and many other) screens over recent weeks. For the sake of world peace, we can only pray that the conflict will end sooner rather than later. But if the story of the Bruce is anything to go by, it may drag on for years.

I cannot imagine what it must be like to fight for one's country against a more powerful oppressor. It must no doubt rank as one of the highest and most inspiring sacrifices that one can make. As far back as I remember, it was stories like those of the Bruce as well as William Wallace which have spurred me to get up again, dust myself down and plough on with a grimace. Sometimes it feels mad to do it. Yet human history has often shown that madness, or daring to dream, can at times make all the difference.

This is a powerful central theme, which I think makes the Bruce even transcend his Scottishness in terms of being the ultimate never-say-die freedom fighter icon. Since I believe in the self-determination of peoples, this is what partly also renders him my favourite historical figure. In this book I've tried to show how he was both formidable and flawed, set to become the unlikely protagonist of a sequence of highly dramatic events which began when the king of Scotland (by many accounts a peaceful and prosperous nation at the time) fell off his horse and died. With all due respect, I doubt that many episodes in other nations' histories lend themselves as easily to stirring, patriotic and chivalric accounts as the events in Scotland immediately following the passing of King Alexander III in 1286, who broke his neck after a nasty fall during a horse ride undertaken during a stormy night (which he had been begged not to undertake).

It was an unexpected demise, one followed by the untimely passing of his sole heir and granddaughter the Maid of Norway in 1290. This in turn sparked off the dramatic events which started with the Great Cause, when the tragic decision was taken to invite the English king Longshanks to choose a successor – which would be a bit like inviting Putin to decide who should rule Ukraine.

Although there were over ten nobles who claimed the vacant Scottish throne, the chief two contestants were the Bruce's grandfather and John Balliol (backed by the Comyns), with John Balliol selected to be crowned king of Scotland in 1292. Yet Longshanks' constant interference in the running of the Scottish kingdom and his treating Balliol as a vassal enraged the Scots, ultimately leading to Balliol being deposed and the subsequent Wars of Scottish Independence in 1296.

It is around this time that William Wallace began his ascent to Scottish national hero, and when we first get a glimpse of the Bruce's patriotic (or ambitious?) leaning. The Bruce went against the wishes of his father (who in his youth was a companion of Longshanks on the Ninth Crusade) when he decided to take up the Scottish cause due to the influence of his grandfather's friends. Yet Longshanks soon crushed Wallace at Falkirk, so that the Bruce and other rebel nobles were forced to surrender to Longshanks at Irvine. There followed a period in which the Bruce became known as one of the leading knights in the known world, who also fought for Longshanks against his own fellow Scots. This no doubt incensed his rival John 'the Red' Comyn, who was John Balliol's nephew and born in the same year as the Bruce.

Yet the Bruce still maintained his kingly ambitions, so that he eventually also entered a secret pact with the Red. The latter probably proceeded to reveal their agreement to Longshanks, so that the Bruce barely escaped London with his life, after being served with a warning (twelve pence and a pair of spurs) by Longshanks' son-in-law Ralph de Monthermer (who was also the stepfather of the Earl of Gloucester). The prologue of this book recounts how a furious Bruce proceeded to attack the Red in a church before being crowned king of Scotland at Scone in 1306. As expected, a furious Longshanks sent Pembroke north at the head of a huge army to crush the Bruce, which Pembroke achieved by means foul at Methven, when practically all of the Bruce loyalists were wiped out.

It is amazing how the king of Scotland was suddenly a wanted outlaw in his own land, with recent screen dramatisations like 2018's 'Outlaw King' revealing the hopelessness of his plight. For over a year he was a fugitive hunted down by the English as well as Scots loyal to the Red. The many anecdotes and stories about how the Bruce went from being a ragged runaway inspired by a spider, to winning his country back castle by castle, still makes for inspiring reading. These stories may have been partly embellished by the chroniclers and poets commissioned by the Bruce after Bannockburn, yet still make for great stories.

As for the Bruce himself: besides being a great and impulsive warrior like his brother Eideard, he was also an impressive guerrilla fighter and ruthless strategist, traits he shared with his best friend the Black Douglas. Yet there was also a stately and highly learned side to the Bruce, which was something he held in common with his nephew Thomas Randolph. I sometimes think, reading through the accounts about the Bruce's life and his three closest commanders, that he was a combination of each of Eideard, Douglas and Randolph, each of them giants in Scottish history who each reflected his different sides. He is also meant to have been a loved and respected ruler in Scotland, known as 'Good King Robert.' His championing of pluralism was not bad for a man of his time: he created a parliament which was far more representative of the full community of his realm, with burgesses from each royal burgh attending sessions for fourteen years after which it became normal practice.

As for his martial capabilities: I could mention how he proceeded to invade England and Ireland himself after Bannockburn, in order to create new fronts against his English enemies. Yet his crowning moment will forever remain the David vs Goliath clash of Bannockburn. In terms of military strategy it remains one of the most tactically astute and innovative victories in military history, which has the Bruce standing tall in the pantheon of legendary freedom fighters. The humiliation suffered by the English was considerable, with author Ronald McNair Scott stating in his book 'Robert the Bruce, King of Scots' that at the end of the battle, the Pelstream and the Bannock burn were *'so choked by struggling men and horses that the latest comers could pass dryshod over a causeway of drowned and drowning bodies.'*

And if the account of the medieval poet Barbour is to be believed, the humiliation suffered by King Edward II after the battle was incredible. He was first denied entry into Stirling Castle by its governor Philip Mowbray, who instantly declared for the Bruce. His party were next stalked by the Black Douglas and his party of sixty Scottish horsemen, who caught up with Edward's troop of five hundred mounted bodyguards beyond Linlithgow, harrying and shadowing them all the way to Dunbar. With the Scots being hot on their heels, the king and his bodyguard were forced to relieve themselves as they rode to safety. They also had to abandon their horses before rushing through the castle gates of Dunbar.

Another aspect of the Bruce's true greatness was his consideration and courtesy towards an enemy which had never shown him or his family a scintilla of mercy. He had the bodies of Gloucester and Clifford sent to their families at his own expense. He also gave thirty-four English barons and several hundred fallen knights and squires an honourable burial in sanctified ground. He treated the hundred captured barons, baronets and knights as guests while their ransoms were arranged. These included the English king's brother-in-law and Gloucester's stepfather Ralph de Montermer (who had warned the Bruce to flee London many years earlier by sending him twelve pence and a pair of spurs). The Bruce delighted in entertaining Ralph at his own table before releasing him without ransom.

Curiously, another captive taken at Bannockburn was a Carmelite friar named Baston, who was tasked by King Edward II to immortalise in verse the English army's expected triumph against the Sots. Upon being brought before the Bruce, the Scottish king promised (with gentle humour) to release the friar if he revised the epic in favour of the Scots.

Yet the greatest catch of all was of course Sir Humphrey, Earl of Hereford and Constable of England, who was taken at Bothwell Castle by Eideard Bruce. It was the capture of Sir Humphrey which enabled the Bruce to demand fifteen Scottish captives, which included his daughter Marjorie, his sisters and of course his wife, Elizabeth de Burgh.

Sydney, Australia
18 March 2022

Acknowledgements

Thanks to everyone at Tearaway Press: Anton, Frank, Josie, Bobby, Menchie, Salli, Rafa, Leila, Dery and Coleen. And anyone else who helped finalise this book and get it out there, you know who you are.

About the Author

James was heralded as 'the new king of historical fiction' by respected British newspaper The Scotsman in July 2022, in the publication's review of James' acclaimed novella *Mad King Robin*, a thrilling story about the famous Scottish king Robert the Bruce.

He was born and raised in Malta, an island nation influenced by thousands of years of imperial history, from the Romans to the British. His burning passion for exciting and dramatic historical events was forged in this environment.

After reading law and history at the Universities of both Malta and Sydney, James qualified as a lawyer and also completed a doctoral thesis on the rights and freedoms of peoples at international law. He subsequently worked for years on editing and publishing content for various multinational government bodies like the European Union as well as US and Australian corporations.

Upon emigrating to Sydney in 2007, James turned his hand to novel writing, crafting dramatic and well-researched stories about various peoples' struggle for freedom.

His debut novel *The Sheriff's Catch* is a highly acclaimed thriller, which recounts the adventures of a Spanish Armada castaway in Tudor Ireland, who joins in the great struggle to liberate western Ireland from brutal suppression. Following its release in 2018, the novel made bestseller lists in Europe and was also named an 'Outstanding Historical' by the IAN Book Awards in 2019, while receiving various other international awards and nominations.

The Sheriff's Catch was recommended as a 'must-read of the week' by leading British newspaper The Yorkshire Evening Post, with global institution Reader's Digest also reviewing it and stating 'while Vella-Bardon's writing displays its own signature, readers will see favourable comparisons with historical fiction greats such as Conn Iggulden, Wilbur Smith and Bernard Cornwell.'

If you enjoyed **MAD KING ROBIN,**

you are sure to enjoy its prequel

THE CREAM OF CHIVALRY, which you

can download for FREE from the author's website.

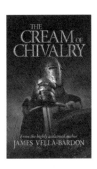

Other titles from the same author

THE SASSANA STONE PENTALOGY

A thrilling, award-winning series which recounts the harrowing

and inspiring adventures of a Spanish Armada castaway and his

adopted rebel tribe in Tudor Ireland.

 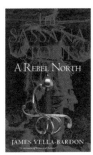 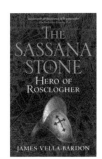

www.jamesvellabardon.com